THE DEVIL'S PLAYGROUND

BOOK ONE OF THE SAPPHIRE STAFF SERIES

CYNTHIA SENS

iUniverse LLC
Bloomington

iUniverse books may be ordered through booksellers or by contacting:

iUniverse
1663 Liberty Drive
Bloomington, IN 47403
www.iuniverse.com
1-800-Authors (1-800-288-4677)

Because of the dynamic nature of the Internet, any web addresses or links contained in this book may have changed since publication and may no longer be valid. The views expressed in this work are solely those of the author and do not necessarily reflect the views of the publisher, and the publisher hereby disclaims any responsibility for them.

Any people depicted in stock imagery provided by Thinkstock are models, and such images are being used for illustrative purposes only. Certain stock imagery © Thinkstock.

ISBN: 978-1-4917-1183-5 (sc)
ISBN: 978-1-4917-1184-2 (hc)
ISBN: 978-1-4917-1185-9 (e)

Library of Congress Control Number: 2013918825

Printed in the United States of America.

iUniverse rev. date: 11/05/2013

This book is first and foremost dedicated to my Mom, for all those moments of being a true mother with your help and loving support.

It is also dedicated to family past and present and finally to Mrs. B—a teacher.

PROLOGUE

"Delgado!" my voice roared with hoarse savagery. My feet plunged into the muddy earth in digging ruts on my pursuit for justice. I told myself I was here to destroy a scientific instrument of immense danger that should never have existed in the world. But really I was here for revenge. "Delgado!" I bellowed.

Men scattered from the observer's stage on the US Army's experimental field in Jonas Valley, New York. The night air was thick and muggy but the fog had lifted enough to see. It was October 1948. I wielded the sapphire staff, a holy instrument. Its power wielded by my hand tossed men about the dark field like refuse in a whirlwind. The bodies and shadows merged with yells of fear and confusion; I had taken them by surprise.

"Captain, what are you . . ?" General Brocke barked as I swung the sapphire staff around causing an army truck to crash onto its side and burst into flames. With each clap of brilliant flaming thunder from the staff, I flung those who would stop me out of my way.

I wasn't interested in the general. I wasn't interested in the bullets now being directed at me. I wasn't interested in my bleeding shoulder or the friends and love I might be leaving behind. I wasn't interested in being labeled a traitor or dying. I was here to destroy the device . . . and I was here to destroy Delgado.

I held the blazing tool of etheric righteousness in my grasp. It was a torch, a weapon; the flash of the sapphire fire contracted my pupils as my eyes shot to the fallen object of my desire. The device had dropped from its inventor's dead hands in the wake of my well aimed strikes and the riotous abandon they had triggered on the observer's stage. It lay now innocent and safe in the protecting mud.

The device's glass face caught the reflection of orange explosions and blue flames. The howling yells and screams were no longer distinguishable; they had merged with the din of gunfire and explosions.

Noxious air, a hot breathy wind born of the inferno I had ignited was sweeping the dark field its demon tongue tasting my fear and feeding on my anger. I saw him now and he saw me, Delgado. His tall form stood amid the chaos. His round opaque glasses always obscuring his cold eyes, stared at me. His senses were trained on the same object as my own. It was the device, the small innocuous clock capable of such disaster and power. The blueprints were gone. The man who had invented it now dead, in a smoking crater, along with those I had already torn through to reach this spot in the field.

The device lay between us. Even behind his obscuring fogged spectacles I knew we were both looking at the same thing. The hot breath of the explosions touched the sweating skin beneath my torn army uniform. Now only the device survived and I was here to make sure that didn't continue.

But now there was a choice. Did I complete the mission and honor my friend's final sacrifice or did I take revenge for my best friend's death and kill Delgado. I swung the flaming blue sapphire staff in a protective circle about me. My eyes darted to the device. I hadn't made it in time. It had been activated. The small metal dials were rotating within its glass cover. My eyes shot to Delgado and saw the barrel of his weapon now aimed at my chest. I didn't fear it. But the device stood between me and revenge, between honor and hatred.

I threw a grenade toward the device. It slid from my fingers with relative ease like all the others. I had no time. I gripped the blazing sapphire staff tighter in my grasp and flung myself onto the live grenade and the active device. If nothing else I wouldn't let Delgado save the object of his desire. I pulled the sapphire staff tight as bullets disintegrated in its azure field; tighter perhaps in hope of protection, perhaps in hope of survival, perhaps just in damn deluded optimistic hope . . . the bastard.

I held the staff surrounding myself, the temporal device and the grenade in an energy of sapphire isolation and separation. My eyes shut. My fingers tightened about the instrument of God's will. I may have prayed. I may have cursed. The grenade inches from my heart ignited just as the device activated. My existence exploded in a cocoon of light, forces greater than the grenade struck my soul as licking flames devoured my body. I had made it through the war. I had made it through more close calls than I could possibly remember and this was how I died, in a dark field, surrounded by enemies on the eve of my best friend's death.

At first a pressure burned to my core, it stabbed at my chest with knives of razors and grated against bone mangling my flesh into unholy shapes. I, a collection of cohesive elements was melting in a crucible of time.

CHAPTER ONE

Millions of burning needles lanced my skin and scorched my senses in a nightmare flash of instantaneous pain. White blinding light became everything then nothing, nothing but consuming darkness. A black that was palpable. I willed my eyelids to open but their muscles were paralyzed and unresponsive to my brain's demands. The searing needles stabbed deeper, deeper until they pierced muscle, sinew, bone; deeper still until I felt them stab my very soul. Suddenly I jolted forward out of the swallowing black into the night, out of the dream and into what I hoped was reality. For a moment I believed I felt cool grass beneath my fingers. Believed I smelled the wet odor of earth that hung in the night as its air invaded my nostrils, then my hands grasped the sweat wrung bed sheets and I remembered. Remembered I was no longer there, no longer in the past. I was at home, in the present, in the future, in bed a thousand miles away from that memory. A memory I knew was no figment of nightmare or of imagining. I was awake and alive.

"Agh . . ." I let out a breath signaling I was still in existence, barely. "Ahh . . ." I moaned with a low guttural tone. I had too many nights like this.

There are two things I need to explain. First I was born in 1916 and it's 2011. No I'm not ninety-five, because the second thing is my age. I'm forty-four years old. Yeah, I know I was never good with math. Weird, but the way my life goes it only gets weirder. You may ask how does something like that happen, being born in 1916 and only forty-four years of age in 2011. When I should be . . . well old . . . a few years shy of one hundred anyway. I could tell you it involves a lot of things, but mostly stupidity, anger . . . and a whole lot of grief. The truth is I really don't have a clue why I'm here. But then I guess cosmically we can all say that . . . why are we here. I don't have the answer and I doubt I ever will. Ok so that was just a little too metaphysical for my brain to noodle, at this time of night or anytime. How I got here well that's what the nightmare had been about . . . what all my nightmares were about.

I inhaled a long breath. I flopped back to the mattress and the fist wrinkled sheets and breathed a shallow sigh of what I guessed was relief. I lay there motionless, staring a moment longer into the placid night. Large puddles of sweat pooling on the surfaces of my skin, my heart slowed finding its rhythm; before I finally swung my legs off the bed and rose to my feet. I didn't bother looking at the clock I knew what time it was, 12:34 a.m. It was always 12:34.

I wandered down the short carpeted hall from my bedroom into my small kitchen, clicking the light on as I went. The bright overhead bulbs, in the circular frosted glass fixture, flashed against my eyes with glaring intensity. I'd barely started across the floor before one of the two light bulbs popped with a sizzling wheeze. I blinked in a wincing fashion. It was a manly wincing all the same. What . . . that made seven bulbs this week . . . higher than average. These nightmares were cutting through my supplies. The stone covered kitchen floor was cold to my feet but it felt good against the sweating heat of my tired body. I opened the old curved lime green fridge. The old thing looked more like a Buick than an appliance and it was about as tough. Its motor purring like a perfectly tuned car as I stood before the exhale of icy air. I shivered slightly, again in a manly fashion mind you; as the hair on my arms and body raised and the remaining sweat on my skin chilled. I really didn't want anything, but finally grabbed a bottle of homemade mead from the two dozen I had just bottled the week before and headed through the living room of my house toward my office.

My living room wasn't a huge area by any means, but it was probably as big if not bigger than my front office. It held an old davenport by the cream painted bedroom wall. The old thing weighed more than my three other comfortable old upholstered arm chairs together. Two of the chairs were age softened leather, worn and cracked in places but still with another couple of decades worth of use to be had. The third chair with its cushioned footstool was upholstered in a natty old green material, similar to a laundered army uniform, that would probably last forever, because it was tougher than iron. There was a small golden coffee table with numerous ring stains on its wooden surface, particularly a red ring that was most likely from wine, giving it a used character I liked. I side stepped it making sure I didn't crack my bare shin against its tapered ledge. But the most prominent feature of the room wasn't furniture at all but a black spiral wrought iron staircase that wound upwards to the second story of my house.

I pushed past the brown dividing curtains to my office. My home and office were divided by thick curtains, of flecked brown fabric, that could be pulled across to separate the two rooms during business hours. They seemed to do their job. My office was a large glorified entryway with partially exposed brick walls. It had enough room for a desk some filing cabinets and furniture. That was if I had any furniture besides the two wooden chairs that sat in front of my old desk. It was more than an office; it was my store front livelihood to the world even though I rarely had the open sign out.

My small two story old brick building wasn't very big but it was stone and solid. Two stories of old style construction when workers cared about their jobs and two by four's actually measured two by four inches; besides the basement of the old building alone had sold me. That and no one else had wanted the old mom and pop store. Originally it had been a dry goods store, built around the turn of the century. That's the nineteenth century since me and centuries have an odd relationship. It was a shoe and clothing store, an insurance company and finally the final indignity it had been split up into miniscule apartments, abused before abandoned and put up for sale. It had taken me months of gutting the shreds of apartment grim, dead mice and squirrel nests, of stripping, cleaning and repair. But she finally felt happy now, happy to be a home.

I tied my robe around me, blocking the cold and sopping up the remaining sweat as I sat down at my worn old wooden desk. Half the finish on its flat surfaces was rubbed away leaving a golden well used patina of hand worn areas and grooved away use. I unsnapped the top of the brown chilled bottle, letting the porcelain white plug dangle against my fingers before taking a needed swig. The taste was

4

mellow and sweet but had a hardy after taste, a good batch if I said so myself. The front windows to the street were dark except for pale shadows cast by the high overhead street lights a few houses down the street. A moment from my nightmare flashed back into my mind. I shook my head and noticed a blinking red light on the edge of my desk. It was the light of my answering machine. I disliked the foul contraptions, especially this new digital one. It unfortunately had become a reluctant necessity; I couldn't be here all the time. Now if the blasted thing worked long enough for me to get a message I might learn to tolerate it. I hesitated as I pushed the tiny round button and waited. I'd already popped a light bulb. What was one more answering machine. I gave a distained glance to the other side of the room. There was already a cardboard box in the corner with two predecessors to the current one that was glaring at me with its red little eye.

"Mr. Taylor?" The voice said my name as if it were a tentative question. "Joseph Morgenstein gave me your name . . . ." There was a long drawn out pause. "Umm . . . ." Another pause as the man stuttered to find his opening. "I don't know if you can help me, but . . . my son . . . Jeffrey . . . he . . . disappeared almost a year ago . . . ."

A little late to be calling me then, I thought taking another swig from the cold bottle as the sweat on my body started to lessen.

"Joseph said, well he told me to call you . . ."

Thanks Joseph.

". . . the police have all but given up . . . . they think, they think he . . . he's just a run away . . . but he didn't run away." The man's statement was emphatic. "I know he didn't . . ." There was another pause.

I could tell just from the man's voice he was at his rope's end and the rope was fraying. The poor guy sounded desperate and he must have been if he was calling me.

"If you could help me I would apprec . . ." he cut off. "I need your help, any help . . . ." There was a deep undertone of pleading sorrow in the man's voice. "Please Mr. Taylor, my name is Isaac Zalbowski, you can reach me at 555-0941 . . . . please . . ." The machine beeped.

I didn't have time to think before the machine made a second beep.

"Mel . . . Melburn are you there?" The second message had started. "It's Joseph . . . pick up if you're there . . ." he waited. "Mel . . ." he waited again. ". . . you may not like this but I gave your name to someone I think you might be interested in . . . or . . . I know . . . anyway his name is Isaac . . . Zalbowski. And just . . . don't shoot me the next time you see me, ok . . ." The machine beeped once more and then paused before the light shut off.

"Thanks Joseph," I said running my hand over my stubbled face and yawning before taking another swig. Joseph was a good friend, hell he was probably my only friend in town. We had hit it off after only the first few minutes of our initial meeting. I'd come to the Midwest just over a year ago and at the time had conversed with no one other than real-estate, bank and general fun contract type people. Joseph was the first actual person I'd befriended . . . or he'd befriended me. I wasn't sure which; we just seemed . . . familiar around each other . . . like old friends. Which hadn't happened to me much in the last few years or decade.

Joseph owned a small independent bookstore and publishing

company. His bookstore consisted of an ever revolving collection of not only his own published works but a myriad of used, rare and unique antiquarian books. While the publishing end specialized in alternative history and science along with a few choice novels Joseph liked, thrown in for good measure. Rounding off his little business empire he also had an environmental lawn service catering to everything from aquaculture to snow shoveling and everything in between. That's right bookstore, publisher and lawn guy. He called the whole thing the Rose Tree. A small topiary red rose bush decorated the end of each spine on his books and his multiple business cards, multiple because he was his own printer. He had three businesses but at last count he had about twelve different business cards.

I had gone into the bookstore that was only a few blocks away from my building and within walking distance on a different street, a few days after purchasing my old derelict building. Its restoration had overwhelmed me and I decided to walk the neighborhood wondering if I could remember anything. I had come from this area years ago, a lifetime ago, but then I had never lived in the city, so reminiscing was a bit of a long shot. I had grown up on a farm and well . . . when I had gotten old enough I'd moved away. Needless to say the neighborhood didn't look anything like it would have if I'd remembered it from nearly seventy years earlier anyway.

Joseph's 'Rose Tree' was in a block of buildings dating from the 1920's. It was on one of the few business streets in this area of town. My old building had gotten lost among the residential houses over the years and now appeared the odd ball among the clabbered single family houses and duplexes. One more reason I'd liked the brick dinosaur. Joseph, however, had taken three different buildings next to each other. Two tall, three stories and a squat one story and remodeled the facade in matching renown, all warm green and bright gold with a bright red rose tree painted on the bookstore's front door. It was quite impressive between the beauty parlor, with its peeling window sign and the blue haired grandmothers who exited it in clouds of permified wonder. On the other side of the Rose Tree was a dingy Mexican restaurant on the corner, which always appeared to be open for business but you couldn't tell if it was or not through the grungy dirt covered windows. The Rose Tree's front windows however screamed to be investigated. The stunted bay windows were filled with dozens of titles that begged to be read. Titles that promised the solved wonders of the ancient Egyptian pyramids, the legends and lore of the Sasquatch, free energy devices, underwater worlds, and Mayan languages, all mingled with the classics of Dante, Verne, Stevenson and Shakespeare as well as organic chemistry, religion and medicine; all woven in what seemed to be endless aisles of shelves and rooms. Joseph had about twenty-four employees in total, not counting the army of teenagers that seemed to renew and change every summer with his lawn service. I had been in luck, that or fortunate to find Joseph that day in the bookstore. He was bustling around putting out new inventory, some new book on lost civilizations. They were lost but that didn't seem to stop people from writing about them. He liked to keep his hands in every part of the business including trimming hedges and mowing lawns with his fleet of rechargeable mowers, on of course the cooler days of autumn.

Joseph had helped me out of a scrap right after I had moved in, a year or so ago, I guess I owed him some help especially after what had happened to his lawn service truck. I hadn't told Joseph a lot of the details about exactly what had happened. Maybe because I didn't remember a whole lot, concussions tend to make you a little foggy on details. I'd rammed his truck into a car going the wrong way on a bridge at midnight, well 12:34 a.m. to be precise. I told you it's always 12:34. It wasn't an accident or anything like that; I meant to run into the car. Hey I stopped the lady I was helping from taking a header into the Mississippi river . . . after I'd had to tackle her . . . when she ran from the car . . . it's a long story. She'd gotten involved with the wrong people in some guinea pig drug trial at the local college. I'd run into her, well met, I ran into her later, when I was doing some research at the college. I'll just say she really wasn't herself that night on the bridge, or for about two or three hours after that. It was a swell time trying to keep her from running out into my street. I'd only let her get away once, and then for just a minute. But somehow she still made it three blocks before I caught her again. Luckily my neighbors hadn't called the cops. She was a quiet runner, not a screamer. I think that had made the difference. Maybe the drug made you faster as a side effect, I don't know. It must have because it took me forever to catch her. I could still feel the ache in my shoulder from that miscalculated tackle on the bridge. I'd tell Joseph the full story sometime, if I remembered it, till then I could help out his friend with the missing kid.

I'd only told Joseph I helped people sometimes nothing more. I mean it wasn't my day job, but then my day job wasn't really my day job. I'd had to tell him something to explain how I had destroyed his truck. Leave it to Joseph to recruit more unsolicited, unpaying and probably difficult work for me. Helping people generally only landed me in more trouble, I say more because there generally wasn't a time when I wasn't having some problem. After all it was one in the morning and I already had two appointments lined up.

I played Mr. Zalbowski's message again and wrote down his telephone number. I'd have to deal with it in the morning. I finished off the mead and headed back to bed, hoping to get some needed rest before tomorrow.

CHAPTER TWO

It was one of those beastly mid-August days where the humidity and heat rose before the sun. I didn't bother shaving. I didn't see the point. I looked in the mirror. The white hairs were starting to replace the black and brown, so far it wasn't too much. The dark hairs were holding the front secure from the encroaching newcomers. But there were even a few stray white ones in my beard now. I brushed my fingers back over my temples and through my hair; at least I wasn't losing any of it. I wasn't the greatest specimen by far but certainly not the worst. I looked better scruffy than I ever had cleaned up, which was good because I often looked scruffy. I was technically ninety-five years old, but I still looked good. Something I never thought I could say at ninety-five . . . I guess time travel had agreed with me.

My hazel eyes stared back at me under a mop of straight uncombed or at least finger combed hair that could have probably used a trim. They were a mix between deep walnut and watery blue as though they couldn't decide which they preferred so they just went with both. I had curving eyebrows that had an unfortunate tendency to express more than I wanted them to say at times; a straight nose that didn't make me distinguished or ugly and when I smiled a snarky kind of grin that often times came out quite goofy looking with the dimpled wrinkles it caused. My stubble was always thicker under my nose and on my chin, making my cheek bones appear broader than they actually were. I was still fit enough that my pants didn't hang below my gut, and still strong enough to extract myself if the situation called for it, which it often did. But overall I was pretty passable; I mean I was . . . ninety-five.

So what does someone as old and yet as young as me do for a living. Well, I made money as a genealogist, at least that's what it said on the door. It wasn't a lot of money, far from it most weeks. It wasn't a band announcing career, which suited me fine. But then my last employer, the US Army, hadn't paid me much either. I guess I was more what you would call a researcher of family legacies officially; but I tended to research a lot more than just families from the records and histories of the past, a past that, to all rights, should have been my own. My profession gave me enough to live on most weeks, not counting what I'd found in my storage unit after fifty years. Not money, but enough things to sell, to make me a decent nest egg. Honestly, I just found people, some of whom probably never wanted to be found. Most of them were dead but that seemed somewhat appropriate given my circumstances. I had reasons for finding them and other things. My reasons for finding them were my own, mostly for my safety as well as theirs.

My first appointment was actually an interview, not of me, but of someone who I might employ. Joseph had been nagging me about the research opportunities of the internet. I kept hearing about it from him, every time I walked into the Rose Tree . . . no matter how much I tried to ignore it. It wasn't something I wanted to consider but . . . they called it progress. I had my doubts. I didn't actually have to do the research myself. I didn't even have to have one of those internet machines in my house; which was probably best. I could, Joseph told me, employ someone to work at home. All the better I thought I didn't want the electronic computing device with its electromagnetic emissions polluting my house. I mean I knew they didn't take up whole floors and use those punch cards anymore like oversized calculators, but I still didn't like them. Besides just being near it I would probably blow it up, or the thing would catch on fire. I wasn't joking. It wasn't just light bulbs that didn't like me. I'd found even simple clocks with batteries tended to short out or start to malfunction after one of my nights of recalcitrant memories, just like the one I'd had last night. It seemed the old metal cased fridge, that sat on the stone floor could take it and the basic electricity of my old brick building appeared for the most part unphased by my combative physiology. Except, of course, for the one day of the year when all bets were off; the same day every October, the day when my nightmares became an all too present reality. But I made damn sure I was away from everything and everyone on that particular day. It made me a danger not only to every other living thing but also to myself. I shuddered slightly just thinking about it.

The bell to the front door pull rang. I pulled out my silver pocket watch, 9:05; so much for punctuality I thought snapping the silver clasp and sliding it back in my pants pocket.

"Miss Porret," I said opening the door, noting the word genealogist on the glass was soon to read eneaolgist. I had enough problems with weirdoes off the street coming in and asking me questions. Like what kind of rocks I studied, I think that particular scholar meant geologist, I didn't need more. I made a mental note to fix it.

"Yeah," she replied with a snap of gum.

I returned her affirmation with a wincing strained smile. I probably would have been smart to slam the door shut, but I didn't. You live and learn or at least I should.

"Please come in, have a seat," I motioned to a set of straight wooden mission style chairs in front of my worn desk. The young woman landed on the chair with all the grace of a cement pillow. I eyed the bright pink flip flop now dangling from the peeling painted large toe nail of her raised foot. Her feet were bare and her gams stuck out a bit like pasty chicken legs from the overly tight cropped jeans that seemed to be causing the enormity of her girth to relocate northward into her ample and equally tightly wrapped cleavage. Had I seen her on the street I would have wagered her office was somewhere near the corner and under a streetlight.

"So what does this job pay?" she questioned brushing her mop of died blonde hair from her dark mascara eyes.

"I haven't hired you yet," I replied thinking of ways I could already end the interview. I had to wonder why she could take the time to put on the black lines to accentuate her eyes but not find anything more than shower clogs for shoes.

"Oh right," she returned and started scavenging in her feed bag that looked as though it had been dragged behind a city bus at some point. "Here," she thrust a crumbled paper at me.

Taking it I smoothed it out, and assumed it was what she called

14

a resume and not a rap sheet. Though I felt it was more a history of disastrous and disappointed employers. I was about to give her the old I'll call to let you know, when a shrieking voice and electric guitar erupted from her bag. She pulled out a miniscule telephone.

"Yeah," she answered. "I can't talk now . . ."

"Yes you can," I said rising from my desk.

"What?" she began, smacking the phone as if that would improve its reception.

It reminded me I needed to block the windows on my office somehow for the cellular signals.

"What . . . ? No I said I left it in the car . . . what . . ." she replied into the phone.

"Thank you," I said pulling her up from the chair. Her hand and phone never coming away from her head as I pulled and pushed her toward the door. It took more effort than I thought it would.

"No the car, your car . . . what?" she replied irritated into the phone as the voice on the other end faded to static.

"Thank you," I said again opening my door and giving her one last shove to the sidewalk. "We won't call."

"Hey . . ." she sputtered, the phone still in her ear, finally realizing I was kicking her out. "Do I get the job or what?"

"Or what," I replied and slammed the door to her mascarded face. Unfortunately the door had a glass window and I could still see her crinkled over shadowed eyelids of miscomprehension, draping her puggish now upturned nose.

"I don't know what his problem is," she continued into the phone. "No it's under the seat, the passenger seat . . ." The pointless conversation continued. I could still hear parts of it even in my

15

retreat until finally a minute or two later she had disappeared from view.

So much for Miss Porret, I said crossing her name off my list for the day.

I grabbed a stack of manila envelopes from the side of my desk, research I had finally finished. It was a week's worth of completed jobs that needed to be mailed out. I also grabbed my old leather bag before heading out for the day to run errands. I closed and locked the front door. The sun was already sizzling on the sidewalk. It was your normal hot miserably humid Midwest day, when the weather couldn't decide between rain and sun, resulting in human lobsters slowly being boiled by the humidity. I noted the enealogist problem was more noticeable with the closed sign behind it and headed around my building for the gravel drive. I was surprised to not see my neighbor Mr. Delmar out to gawk in his normal unabashed fashion. His railed porch was empty.

I pulled a large glass bottle of water from my worn leather wide mouth bag and opened the fuel flap on my brown beast, a 1941 Chevrolet Fleetline. Its smooth curving surface heated by the hot sun. Its hawk like hood stood above the rounded fenders, each with silver circled ball headlights that stared out over the impressive silver grill and bumper. She was one of the first four door models. I had picked her up at a used car lot in upper New York State in early 1948. She had barely run when I first found her. I don't know what the previous owner had done to her, but because she was in such bad shape I got her for a song. Fifty years later I found myself living in my storage unit and sleeping in the back seat of the brown beast. It took me months to rip the engine out and reengineer it using papers and sketches that an old friend had given me. She meant a lot to me, the brown beast; we had been through quite a bit together. I had spent long hours with her, talking to her about what had happened, about the things and people I'd lost, whether I was lost, whether I was crazy. You would think talking to a car would have given me a definite answer as to my sanity but alas . . . it was more therapy than work. Getting her cleaned enough to run had kept me busy during those awkward early years of transition from 1948 to 1998.

I deposited the water, which was enough fuel for the day. The clear liquid ran into the tank with satisfying glugs. I tossed the empty bottle on the floor of the back seat and rolled down the window as I got in the driver's seat. She purred to life with one wheezing pop and then silence, only the gentle vibration of the moving hidden mechanized engine told me she was running. Vincent McMillian was right. He had given me the plans for the engine almost seventy years ago. He'd said the engine would probably run for a hundred years before it needed work. That was so long as I kept the water tank full and gave her a good pat down as Vincent had put it. His terminology was always somehow equestrian related, probably because he fancied himself a cowboy even though he was British and had never been farther than the continent. I don't even think he'd ever been on a horse and his M20 motorcycle didn't count. The unfinished bits and parts I'd removed from the brown beast's chassis had sat incomplete for fifty years. When I'd finally finished her, she had started on the first try of the engine. Who could ask for more, I thought pulling out of my gravel drive.

I dropped the post off and headed out of the cities. The cities, as I called them since they were a collection of average to small sized towns all somewhat clumped together. You quickly passed from one to another without much thought; even with the Mississippi river separating many of the towns from each other on the great divide that marked the woodlands of the east and the prairies of the west. The towns and cities felt connected in a way only someone who lived here could explain. Had one of the individual cities developed into something larger than one of the others somewhere else they might have become boroughs or suburbs. But none had, not here. This was the Midwest, where people liked the feel of small towns and communities. They still valued a sense of individualism and independence even if they didn't always assert it.

Past the highways and onto the farm roads I drove, where the dust from the gravel whipped up a moving trail behind the car in billowing clouds that lingered for long stretches over the countryside in the humid air. I passed cornfield after cornfield. Tall stocks swayed in the breeze as small colored advertisement sign after sign zipped past announcing logoed ownership more than branding. They weren't farmers anymore they were company men, owned and controlled by multinational corporations whose bottom line was profit not produce. I shook my head remembering when families owned these fields not companies. Oh sure people still had the titles but now they were beholden to other company men who wanted to patent life. If they couldn't patent it they'd do their best to control it. Now there were just a few enormous farms sustained with chemicals and genetic modification all growing one single identical crop. It was plant eugenics nothing less. A lot of farmers and families had lost.

'They want to do to people what they do to plants.' The words were an old friend's. Maybe it was a good thing he didn't live to see it, I thought tightening my grip on the steering wheel, maybe. I shook my head again, no it wasn't; he should have lived. If anyone should have he should have.

I turned onto a gravel road flanked by grassy prairie fields that darted with birds and insects under the long blue sky. The sight lightened my mood a bit, pushing the old memories away as I came closer to my destination. Hollow Tree Farm, an oasis in the modern industrial monoculture of farm fields. They had been organic before organic was even a word. Family owned for five generations with no sign of losing it. Financially Brandon and Tabitha Forrester were doing better now than their parents and grandparents.

I drove the brown beast slowly down the drive. Tabitha greeted me with a tall wave as she saw my familiar brown car pull up to the farm house. The recently painted white clabbers of their house shown with brilliance in the hot sun. It was a tall two story with a dormered third floor and shuttered windows.

"Didn't think you'd be here this early," Tabitha said with a smile under her broad straw hat. Her worn blue overalls were rolled up to accommodate the humidity and her bare arms glistening with perspiration. Tabitha was one of the healthiest and happiest people I had ever met. Her skin was bronze, her muscles taut and her smile as wide as the open sky above Hollow Tree Farm. "Brandon's out in the fields . . ."

"I'll see him next time," I replied at the mention of her husband. "I came to see you anyway."

"You did . . ." she gave a warm laughing smile. Her perfect teeth flashed like pearls. "Brandon will like to know that . . ."

"We don't have to tell him," I returned with a goofy smile.

"Oh come on now," Tabitha said. "Before we cause a scandal," she turned waving for me to follow. I headed after her into the shade of the front porch. Pausing as she slipped off her mud covered old shoes and deposited them with a row of others in varying sizes lined neatly on the porch. The screen door squeaked with a familiar reassurance that all screen doors have.

"I see your neighbors across the way haven't changed their minds." I had seen a series of company seed signs on the way down the road.

"No," Tabitha returned with a sigh. "You know he actually told Brandon he knew the corn he grows is crap. He wouldn't eat it himself but he makes a profit so what does he care . . . he actually said that . . ." she sighed again with disgust.

"Well, profit is the name of the game," I answered.

Tabitha stopped and turned with a frown. "There's more to live for than profit. We wouldn't change even if it meant we could only do enough for ourselves, even if we lost the farm."

"That will never happen."

"I know but . . ." she started, removing her broad brimmed hat to reveal golden hair pulled back in a wavy pony tail. Stray long curls ribboned her pink sun warmed cheeks. She tossed her hat in one of the living room's comfortable chairs as we moved toward the kitchen at the back of the house.

"But you have principles, ethics . . ." I added with an acknowledging smile and an arching eyebrow. The white walls and wooden floors always seemed to shine with a warm glow. Items of a loving family graced the rooms. Family pictures, children's drawings, books and toys surrounded me in every direction, the place felt like a familiar happy home in everyway.

"Mommy," a unisoned proclamation called out as two young twin boys of about seven skidded across the polished wooden floor in their socks. "Hello Mr. Taylor." They both greeted together coming to a halt in the doorway that led off to the rest of the house.

"Hello boys," I always twinged slightly when I saw the twins. They were blonde like their mother with cherubic young faces that shone like little suns. My reaction had nothing to do with them. It had to do with the fact that they were twins. Tabitha always noticed it but had never said anything.

"Boys back to your schoolwork," she shushed with a loving wave.

"Yes ma'am," they returned in unison again before disappearing into the other room; a series of giggling and playful banter trailing them.

"They grow like weeds those two, shoot up an inch I think overnight."

"They do that," I said still somewhat numb to her words. When I finally turned to face her I realized she was staring at me.

"What is it about those boys?" Tabitha questioned looking at me with a kind quizzical frown.

I opened my mouth to speak but couldn't. What could I tell her.

"It's not my place to ask . . . you saved their lives, that's all I need to know . . ." Tabitha smiled with a mother's pat on my arm.

I wanted to explain. It was after all her boys that had pulled me back to my old home town. I had known Brandon's family a lifetime ago at a time, well a time that had changed my life forever. So when I saw that Brandon Forrester's boys were missing, I couldn't stay away. I had to help. I had to stop it from happening again like it had happened to my brother.

"I even made you an apple pie," Tabitha said as we stopped at the bottom of the stairs in front of the row of deep freezers. The Forrester's kept themselves well stocked from their farm all through the Midwest winter. "Just let it thaw completely, then cook it as you normally would . . . I put an instruction note on top."

"Thanks Tabitha," I returned with a gracious smile. When I came to help the Forrester's I had never expected to become such good friends with them. But I quickly found myself not only drawn to visit them, just to make sure everything was fine; I soon found myself needing their help. Their farm sustained me, supplying nearly all of my food. Tabitha seemed delighted to include me as one of the family. She was always offering more than I needed like apple pies and bread or cookies. It felt nice to be part of a family again . . . it had been a very long time.

We loaded up the brown beast with the two large coolers. One filled with frozen meats, sauces, home-made pastas made with grains grown and ground right on the farm, and of course the apple pie. The other cooler was filled with fresh vegetables and fruit, mostly berries and summer apples.

"You know you don't have to wait until you need food to visit . . ." Tabitha said, a gentle smile across her lips.

"I know . . . but I don't want Brandon to get jealous or anything." She laughed.

I didn't think Brandon had anything to worry about. Tabitha and Brandon weren't two people who would or could ever be broken apart under even the worst circumstances. I could say that because

I had met them under the most horrendous circumstances; the disappearance of their twin boys, Kevin and Kyle. I shook on old memory from the cobwebs of my mind and remembered I needed to call Joseph's friend Mr. Zalbowski.

"Mel?"

I looked to find her genial features quizzically pondering my thoughts.

"I'm ok," I replied. "Just remembering things I need to do . . ." I gave her another goofy assuring smile.

"Don't be a stranger . . ."

"I won't," I promised, standing next to the brown beast.

"Goodbye Mel," Tabitha said. She was still smiling as she gave me a hug before I got in the car.

That was one of those extra things she threw in that made me always come back. I waved one last time as I pulled down the drive. She returned my wave from the porch. The two boys were bouncing up and down and waving while they hugged close to their mother. I couldn't help a smile. The Forrester's and Hollow Tree Farm held a special place for me, something from an old life long forgotten and lost.

CHAPTER THREE

I pulled into my gravel driveway by mid afternoon and parked next to the sun warmed red brick of my old building. I grabbed the frozen food cooler first and headed for the front door. I noticed a blue Volkswagen parked under the shade of a locust tree down the street. There was someone in the front seat but I couldn't make them out in the shadows. I unlocked my front door, noting the enealogist again and pushed the first cooler inside before heading back to the car for the other. The back door would have been a closer way to the kitchen but my neighbor, Mr. Delmar, tended to stare at anything and everything I did at my back door. I didn't see him but I soon heard his lawn mower making its meticulous and repetitive passes on the opposite side of his house. I quickened my pace and headed for my front door before Mr. Delmar rounded his house. If there was one thing that man loved over watching me, it was mowing his postage stamp of a yard for more hours than there were blades of grass in his lawn. My eyes checked the blue Volkswagen again as I came back from my car the second time. The driver was nowhere to be seen. Maybe they had just leaned over, no need to get paranoid I thought pushing the other cooler inside. There were lots of other people that lived on this street. I locked the front door behind me all the same, and flipped on the lights. The bulb in the lamp by my desk popped with a loud snap and burnt out.

"Great," I said pushing one cooler with my foot as I carried the other one toward the kitchen at the back of my house. I left the vegetable cooler upstairs and heaved the frozen one downstairs. My old enamel lined deep freeze was at the far corner of the basement as I came downstairs from the kitchen. The brick walls of the old basement were still in good shape and a cement floor had been poured over the original earthen floor some time in the past. I had erected some dividing walls to cordon off certain areas making rooms where once small brick alcoves for storage had been constructed. I heard the whoosh of one of the wind fans for my plants begin, as I placed the last of the food in the freezer, then went to inspect.

My second water motor, another genius design of Vincent McMillian, was running silently. Lucky for me, McMillian's small motors ran on a siphon suction form of water power, which meant no electricity was needed. The bright sun lights burned in the plant alcove, reflecting off the mirrored surfaces with blinding efficiency. I kept my distance so they wouldn't go out . . . green foliage of varying hues and shapes fluttered in the artificial breeze. Once years ago the curving archwayed alcoves that lined the northeastern wall had probably been bins for coal but now they served a better purpose as grow rooms for herbs and plants mostly used for medicinal or scientific pursuits. The fan to the poppy alcove had kicked in and the gentle sway of the large white flower heads was beautiful in their gentle graceful dance. It wasn't as dramatic as seeing them in the warm honey brown soil of the Kush; where they were sometimes chest high and the flowers as big as dinner plates while the seed pods grew as large as apples. Their massive fields were like something from a fairy tale under the clear azure sky; but that memory was from decades ago, now more than half a century . . . during a war . . . during a different life. I shook my head, pulling my thoughts back to the present. I checked the water in the three other alcoves, everything was doing fine. I had never been one for plants or medicine. Those had been the interests of others near and dear to me, but necessities arose and Vincent McMillian wasn't the only person who had given me manuals and journals that now proved to save my very life.

I grabbed a spare bulb from the crate of light bulbs on my storage shelf before going back upstairs.

"Hello?" I heard a soft inquiring female voice calling from the front of the house. "Hello? Is anyone . . ."

"How did you get in here?" I growled entering the kitchen and nearly dropping the light bulb on the counter; finding a young woman peering in from my living room as she cautiously inched into my kitchen. I paused momentarily with a slight goldfish expression at her rather fresh beauty. She was standing in my house, bold as brass dressed in jeans and a loose silk blouse the color of a purple sunset or a nasty bruise. Her dark auburn hair came just to her shoulders in curving waves about her heart shaped features and her light blue tennis shoes stood out against my dark stone floor.

"Your door was open," she answered in a blunt matter of fact tone that was more defensive than surprised. No doubt due to my rather aggressive question.

"Open?" I pushed past her so suddenly she didn't have time to move. "You always barge into people's homes without invitation?" I said running to the open front door and not waiting for an answer or excuse which I think she had started. I knew I had locked the front door. I had. Hadn't I? I looked down the street the blue Volkswagen was gone. Crap.

"I'm here about the job," she returned finally getting my attention and straightening her shoulder more from the insult than my actual push.

"What job?" I growled again shutting the door and making sure I locked it. I turned to see the young woman raising an eyebrow at the lock. Ok, granted it might have seemed a little predatory.

"This job," she said holding up a bright orange flyer.

"Joseph," I grumbled recognizing his handiwork and his favorite print type. When had he . . . ?

"You are Mr. Taylor?" she questioned, her eyes shifting to the locked door before falling back on me.

I nodded with a grunt.

"Is there a job?" she questioned as politely as she could still eyeing the locked door behind me. Given I was about 5'11 and in good shape, I could see how my action could be taken. Yet I got the impression trying to stop her from exiting would harm me far more than I might ever be able to harm her.

"Yes . . . there's a job . . ." I paused. ". . . why don't we make an appointment . . . for when things are a little less . . ."

"Weird," she returned. She was calm about my enraged behavior. I'd give her that, calm or defensively restrained.

"Yeah," I grabbed a pencil and a piece of paper from my desk allowing her free and unfettered passage to the door if she so desired.

"Your flyer says I can do this work from home," she said almost with question. "That is true?"

"My flyer . . ." Joseph, I thought. "Yeah . . ." I answered.

"So . . . when would you like to have this interview?" she questioned, her tone softer, her steely blue eyes wide. Her features raised in polite interest. "Might we have it now?"

"What the hell," I returned gesturing to a chair. "I apologize Miss . . ." I began heading for the seat behind my desk. I felt it made me less threatening if there was a desk between us.

"Haptonstall, Emily Haptonstall."

"Hapton . . ." I got half way through the name before my backside hit the chair. I hadn't heard that name in more than sixty years.

"Haptonstall," Emily replied eyeing me. Thinking maybe I hadn't caught it all.

I put my hand over my shocked expression and held my jaw. "Umm . . . umm . . ."

"This would be where you ask me questions . . ." she offered handing me a crisp paper from somewhere on her person. It hadn't been folded so I was slightly alarmed to know where she had it hidden, since she had no purse or bag with her.

"Questions," I stammered.

She nodded. Her eyes staring at me as a slight jovial expression crossed her lips.

"Umm . . . have you ever done any research before?" I was looking at her more closely now, her blue eyes questioning. I was trying to find some resemblance perhaps, or something that would tell me it couldn't be true.

"Yes as you can see I was a librarian for several years and I worked as a reporter for the local Argus for several as well."

"You were a reporter?" I fluttered with astonishment. What were the chances.

"Yes, I've also worked in offices. I have my own computer as was your requirement," she pointed once again to Joseph's flyer. "I need a part time job . . . that I can work from home and . . ."

"Have you lived here all your life?" the question rather bluntly interrupted her . . . which it was odd I grant you but I had to know.

"Yes . . ." Emily returned tentatively and paused, her own eyes seeming to study me.

"Um . . . umm . . . you're hired," I blurted out not quite believing my own response.

"I am . . . you're sure?" she asked looking doubtful, thinking that I might be some sort of crazy person; which some days she wouldn't be too far from right.

"Yes," I answered.

"And the pay, ten dollars an hour . . ."

"Ten!" I exclaimed.

She pointed to the flyer.

"Ten?" Joseph. "Ten."

"Good," Emily replied as I continued looking at Joseph's flyer dumbfounded. "When do I start?"

"Ten," I repeated under my breath. "Start . . . umm . . . tomorrow at . . . ten . . ."

"Good," she returned and rose from the chair. "I will see you tomorrow then . . . thank you, Mr. Taylor."

I nodded still clutching the bright orange flyer. I heard her unlock the front door but by the time I looked up the door was closing and she was already walking down the sidewalk. I wasn't sure what had just happened. Had someone broken in? Had she broken in? Had I just hired the person that had broken in . . . was she driving the blue Volkswagen . . . no it had disappeared. I looked at the closed door. She said her name was Haptonstall. I inhaled and rubbed my finger across my eyes. I had just been struck in the face by a name from my past . . . a wonderful name that had belonged to a wonderful woman. I looked out the window again to the passing traffic. What had just happened?

CHAPTER FOUR

An hour later, after getting over my initial shock of somehow being violated by some unknown entity or criminal, I, for some reason, ok one reason, couldn't believe it had been the woman I had just hired. Probably because I couldn't believe anyone named Haptonstall would ever do me harm. I had called Mr. Zalbowski and made an appointment to meet. Double checked the house to prove to myself whatever had happened was just in my mind, making doubly sure the unlocked door and the Volkswagen phantom were just that, something in my mind. With nothing missing I placed it behind me and headed out. I was going to find Joseph before meeting Zalbowski. I triple checked my locks first then headed for the Rose Tree.

❧❧

"Hello Joseph," I announced entering the Rose Tree bookstore and pulling another orange flyer from the cork board by the door as I came in. The bookstore was rows and rows of shelf lined walls and book cased

31

isles straining under thousands of titles, hard cover, soft cover, spiral bound, heck there might have even been a scroll or two tucked away somewhere among the shelves. Some of the titles were not to be found in any other place. Used and new books interspersed the rows in puzzle like stacks and lines. Books on any and every subject imaginable that was within the alternative, archaeological, conspiratorial framework of Joseph's informational bent, which as far as I could see meant just about anything and everything. Large displays announced the newest published titles of the Rose Tree's publishing works just next door.

"Mel . . . Melburn did they help?" Joseph questioned. His thin frame bounced out from behind the counter. The biggest thing about Joseph was his shock of dark thick hair. It had a more robust body than he did. It coiffed up often times quite high making his face seem longer than it really was. He was younger and shorter than I was and on occasion tended toward bouts of almost nervous anxiety which was probably what gave him the energy to run three businesses at such a young age. Of course it may have been the three businesses that made him so anxious.

"How many of these did you put up? I saw two more on street posts on the way over," I half grunted waving the flyer with a disapproving crinkle of my eyebrow.

"A few," he returned innocently.

I glanced at him.

"A few dozen," he admitted with a shrug.

"Dozen!"

"Did they help?" he questioned ignoring my exclamation.

"Well you can rip them down," I grumbled.

"Why?" he questioned almost in protest. He was probably tired of hearing me complain about having too much paperwork. Who likes paperwork.

"I hired someone."

"From the flyer?" Joseph asked with an overly hopeful tone.

"Yes," I answered reluctantly.

"Ha," Joseph replied with a little too much glee I thought. "Ok, ok I'll have one of the kids rip them down in an hour or so," he motioned with an acknowledging wave, trying to hide a satisfied smile.

"You had them put them up didn't you?"

"Maybe," Joseph answered with coy avoidance.

"Joseph?"

"Yes, but it worked didn't it."

I rolled my eyes and didn't answer. "I called Zalbowski," I said not letting him have another moment to triumph.

"I didn't know if you could help him or not," Joseph answered in a slightly more sheepish tone, looking at me.

"I won't know until I talk to him."

"It was just . . . he said something about his kid being sick and I thought . . . well remember what we were talking about the other night. The fact that these viral inoculation programs can be covers sometimes for test subjects."

I remembered Joseph had occasion when a new author or book passed his desk to delve a little deeper than most people would into a subject.

"When I asked him when his kid got sick and he said after he took him to the clinic . . . for an inoculation . . ." Joseph put the last word in air quotes. "But now the clinic is closed . . . and the kid's gone missing . . . well . . . I thought of you . . ."

"Thanks Joseph . . ." I snarked.

"Sorry," he returned. "But you always say . . ."

"What clinic?" I asked since this was the first I'd heard of it.

"Some free medical clinic off Locust the school told him about . . . I checked it out the building's empty, but you can see where the sign on the door use to be."

"When was this? I mean when did the kid go . . ." I questioned already starting to get pulled into the kid's story.

"I don't know exactly, a month before he went missing . . . my question is, there had to be more than one kid besides Jeffrey right . . . if it was a drug trial or something . . ." Joseph's face became focused in concentration. "The kid was happy . . . no real problems, no bullies, a loving home . . . no reason to run away . . . but nobody else's kids have gone missing. At least that I know of, or from the same school . . . that's why they say he ran away . . ."

"That's because they found the one they wanted," I darkly returned, a justifying anger starting to burn in my gut. I had seen these kinds of things before, and too many times. It was different than the Forrester's but it smelled just as bad.

"They?" Joseph questioned.

"Whoever took the kid . . . somebody took him or he'd have been found by now . . ." I replied.

"Seriously . . . I'm right!" he returned with surprise. "Hey . . . so do you want me to come with you?" Joseph looked at me with an almost hopeful query.

"No . . ." I replied a little too quickly, but recovered with another question. "How well do you know Zalbowski?"

"Not well, I met him at the synagogue."

"Synagogue?" I raised an eyebrow. Joseph wasn't exactly devote when it came to religion.

"I take my mother like any good son would do," he returned ignoring my snark and combing his fingers through his thick hair.

"How is your mother?"

"Better, that stuff you told me about really helped. She wanted me to thank you. Said I should invite you to dinner."

"Dinner," I returned.

"Yes, you know that big meal at the end of the day . . ." he chuckled. "But I told her you had special dietary requirements."

"You make me sound like an endangered species or ailing lab animal."

"Aren't you?" Joseph questioned, stacking some more books on the counter as we talked.

"In a way," I mumbled to myself. "Tell your mother I'd be happy to have dinner with you."

"You would," he gawfed, straightening the books and turning to look at me.

"Don't sound so surprised. I know what common courtesy is Joseph."

"Ok," he replied with some delight.

ஒஇ

I got the address of the medical clinic from Joseph and decided to check it out before meeting Zalbowski. I rolled along Locust street past the myriad of tiny strip malls with varying dollar stores all promising the best deals on cheap plastic crap. That was one of the things I still hadn't gotten use to . . . plastic. It was everywhere. It use to be when you bought something it was first built to last and second you would use it until it was gone and then use it a little longer. But now people bought something one week and the next they were back to buy the same thing or something new and throw out the 'old.' I didn't get it. We were lucky to have what we had and we used what we had forever. Chalk it up to one more thing I no longer understood.

I continued driving until I came to the correct address. The parking lot that stretched out in front of the long multiple divided strip building was crowded with cars, cars unlike mine that were also made mostly of plastic. Again I didn't see the advantage, my brown beast was seventy years old and she was still going, probably better now than when she was made, granted I had made some alterations to the car over the years but the solid body of the old girl hadn't changed. I pulled to the end where a half faded sign in the window declared the empty corner space for rent.

Joseph was right. I could still make out the letters of Midwest Medical Clinic that had once adorned the front window. I parked the brown beast and strolled toward the store front. I could see waves of heat coming off the pavement in the distance. I wiped a bead of sweat away and peered through the dusty window. The rooms were empty. Indented squares and small stains littered the grayish blue berber and unplugged stray telephone wires were all that was visible for office remnants. I'd say from the look of it, the clinic had been closed for some time. I glanced next door. It was a sandwich shop. I took the chance someone might remember something and headed inside. It was well after noon and there appeared to be a lull in business, if the place ever had business. A young man jumped down from his seated position on the counter as I stepped up to the register.

"What would you like sir?" he half sniffed with a lack of enthusiasm that even seemed lacking.

"Information," I returned.

The young man took a frowning moment, as if he didn't remember that item being on their menu. "Oh . . . you go out the parking lot and turn left . . . go until you see the exit," he returned without pause.

I raised an eyebrow.

"The highway ramp, right?" the young man questioned adjusting his baseball cap with the company logo on it. Baseball caps were another thing I didn't understand. Everybody wore those now too, like they had all been drafted to the league. Hats were hats with full brims that went all the way around your head not just stuck out in the front. They were hats not something a little kid would wear.

"Not exactly," I replied. "Next door . . . the medical clinic . . . do you remember anything about it?"

"Can't say I do . . . I've only been here a few months . . ."

"Well has anyone else been here longer?"

"Ah . . . yeah Billy," he answered.

I waited expecting he knew that meant I might want to converse with Billy. I raised an eyebrow.

"Oh . . ." he returned, a light, a very small light, dawning on him. "Billy," he hollered toward the back, quickly realizing I wasn't there for the food. Besides the wilted slices of anemic tomatoes slowly drying out in the metal trays weren't enticing me.

"What?" came a barked answer from the back room.

I assumed the other young man with the pudgy midriff was William. His nose was bulbous and his glasses thick. I pondered a minute what the intense redness of his nose might mean but decided I was better off not guessing.

"Do you remember the medical clinic next door?" I questioned as he stepped toward the counter near the wilted lettuce and shriveled sliced onions.

"Yeah," he returned looking at his fellow employee with question. I wondered if it took both of them to make one sandwich.

"When did it go out of business?" I asked.

He shrugged. Scratched his head through his baseball cap and answered. "Don't know . . . maybe a year ago . . . why?"

"Do you remember anybody that worked there?"

He shook his head. I was beginning to think the baseball caps hid empty hollow craniums beneath them.

"Anything? Do you remember anything?" About the clinic I should have clarified, the strain might be too great for him to try and recall everything.

His face gave a look of sincere indifference or gas. They both stood there silent, entranced lemmings who'd lost the direction to the cliff. I would have said it was apathy, but apathy denoted caring at sometime. This guy was barely firing a single cylinder.

"Thanks anyway gentlemen . . ." I said and turned for the door. I wasn't getting anything out of them but a headache.

"Hey . . . don't you want a sandwich?" the first one asked.

I shook my head. I'd see what I could find out elsewhere.

As I exited the sandwich shop leaving Bill and Bill Jr. slack jawed and staring. I noticed a blue Volkswagen at the far end of the parking lot. Now being the paranoid yet slightly stupid person that I tend to be I headed for the little cerulean bug. I didn't like coincidences and the odds of an old blue Volkswagen in the exact same color and model parked not far from me for the second time today wasn't making my gut feel better, especially not after the sandwich shop. This little favor for Joseph was evolving into something . . . something that was beginning to make my senses twitch.

I made a looping path around the parking lot. So I could avoid any detection. I slinked by a large pick up; nearly swallowing my tongue when a giant barking German shepherd jumped at me from behind the truck's passenger window. I shushed him. He gave me a pleading look. The half open window wasn't enough in the heat. His tongue lolled drool along the outside of the window's glass. He gave a pleading whine.

"Sorry pal . . ." I half offered in a mumble, keeping my eyes focused on the Volkswagen bug.

There was definitely someone in the Volkswagen. I paused a minute. Ok maybe this wasn't such a good plan. They could have guns or muscles . . . or guns . . . guns were worse. But it was too late I was already moving toward the car, the big dog watching me from the truck.

I reached the small Volkswagen and ripped the door open. Thankfully the door was unlocked.

"Why are you following me?" I bellowed in a loud menacing low tone that sought to intimidate and belittle. It was met with a sharp piercing scream. The startled horrified face of an elderly woman, who'd just gone out for a fun shopping day greeted me. I stumbled backwards thankfully staying upright and quickly trying to apologize. The dog now barking from the nearby truck, angered no doubt by the fact I'd opened the door for the little old lady and not for him.

The elderly woman in her purple shirt and spiky white hair didn't wait. She focused her red glass framed eyes at me with vengeance. She continued screaming and hurled her hand bag at me like a bowling ball. It weighed about the same. It struck me in the head. I cursed forgetting for a moment to apologize while she pummeled me.

"I'm sorry . . . I thought . . ." my protests made little effect.

"You horrible man . . ." she shrieked retrieving her millstone of a hand bag once again and striking me repeatedly as the adjacent dog egged her on with encouraging growls. She might have looked elderly. The kindly old grandmother, but she threw swings like a boxer. I dodged two swings but the purse clipped me in the side of the head before I was able to make a full retreat.

I didn't wait around. The parking lot was busy and the woman's howling beratements, accompanied by the barking dog and now a car alarm from somewhere, were quickly drawing onlookers and larger more menacing ones than the little old lady that was thrashing me. I didn't fancy tangling with any of them.

I made it to my car and out of the parking lot before there was any more of an incident. My ear throbbed all the way across town to the records office. I'd calmed down some before climbing up the large stone steps of the courthouse and going inside to see what I could find out about the Midwest Medical Clinic. Making sure I held the door for every elderly woman I saw. I didn't need another beating. I didn't think my ego or head could take it. Needless to say I didn't plan on confronting anyone else in a blue Volkswagen anytime soon. I'm sure it was just . . . I was just over thinking . . . maybe under thinking the way my head was smarting.

ಲ320

"Hold it right there," said a slow deep voice as I came through the cool marble mezzanine of the courthouse out of the blistering heat.

"Oh come on Craig . . . I've only got a few minutes . . ." I returned not needing to see who had just stopped me, Craig Burksen one of the courthouse security guards. He wasn't a cop but he fancied himself one. I didn't argue since he had a gun. I missed the old days when you could actually walk into a building without being frisked at the door.

"Empty your pockets . . . you know the drill."

I rolled my eyes and sighed as he pulled his thumbs from the leather belt about his waist. He was a big guy; burly where it counted with a little extra weight for added force and intimidation. From the thickness of his neck and shoulders I figured he'd played football in his youth, certainly nothing daintier.

"You never find anything . . ." I said rubbing my smarting ear once more as I dropped my keys before him in the tray.

"Hey last time you snuck through the metal detectors when I wasn't here . . . it took them three weeks to get this thing to work again . . . you're not going near it. Empty your pockets and spread them . . ." he motioned to the wall away from the metal detector.

"You'd think I was a common criminal," I returned but complied with his demanding request.

"You are," Craig returned as two other people passed through the metal detector without incident, both eyeballing me as they went.

Ok so I'd destroyed the metal detector a couple of times before Craig caught on I was the reason the thing was going crazy. After that I'd only shorted out and blown up two of his metal detecting wands. I told him not to use them. So now I was subjected to, the far less humiliating, physical pat downs by Craig every time I came in the courthouse.

"Satisfied?" I questioned as he handed me back my keys. "Or do you want my shoes this time too . . ."

"Don't push your luck Mel," Craig returned. "Make sure you don't sneak through the metal detectors . . . I've told everyone this time . . ."

Swell I thought now I get to be groped by a string of second rate security guards every time I come here and all without dinner and a movie.

"Go on," Craig motioned me past. Sticking his thumbs back in the top of his belt and nodding to people as they slipped through the detectors without so much as a faint beep. I envied them.

Whatever I'd done to the metal detectors must have ticked Craig off, because he hadn't even bantered with me which he normally did. I could only imagine the headaches three weeks of malfunctioning detectors had caused him. I shrugged and headed for the records department on the basement floor. I'd have to make it up to him somehow

The area in the basement of the courthouse was the place where records came to languish. The room smelled of dust and paper, old and used and oddly of enchiladas. A large counter with an upper metal gate gave all a decidedly somber welcome as you walked in. Due to county budget problems only one person worked in the basement records archive compared to the upstairs records where all the newest paperwork was filed, stamped and officiated.

"Hello?" I called into the wide empty chasm of the cage.

"Mel . . . is that you?" I heard a call back with an expectant and excited note.

"Who else," I returned still looking around.

"I haven't seen you in awhile . . ." a short women with a bright red shirt emerged from somewhere behind the cage. Her hair was dark and about as wide as her shoulders. The tight thin belt wrapped around her waist gave her the unfortunate appearance of two sausage casings strung together.

"Hi MaryAnn," I smiled. MaryAnn Martinez was a sucker for my smile. I'd found that out right away, the very first time I'd stepped into her parlor of archival madness. She was older than me by a good ten or fifteen years . . . I should clarify. My physical age not my birth age because if it had been my birth age her unwarranted attention would be bordering on Methuselahistic harassment. I shook my head and pulled my thoughts back to MaryAnn . . . but that didn't seem to stop her from pulling out all the stops to see if she could attract my attention. I noted an extra undone button on her red blouse and the more than ample cleavage now being displayed as she came to the counter. I had no doubt she had only just readjusted her clothing for me.

"Hello Mel," she returned with a smile that reminded me of someone trying to ply extra sweets from a candy jar.

I didn't mind. MaryAnn was harmless at least I hoped she was. I never wanted to get locked in her cage and find out. I pretty much just chalked her oversexed behavior up to long hours spent in caged isolation in the sub-basement without human contact other than me and maybe a mail clerk, who I felt really sorry for . . . the poor guy.

"Hello," I returned.

"Something I can help you with . . ." she batted her eyes.

"Need some property information . . . mind if you let me in your cage . . ."

"I never mind," MaryAnn returned with a bobbing motion and another candy smile. "It's letting you out that's the problem."

"What would Mr. Martinez say?"

"Not a thing," MaryAnn said setting the picture of her husband face down on her desk. "He's in Las Vegas with a bunch of show girls . . ."

"You mean your daughter," I returned.

"You're just no fun Mel . . ." she chided, eyeing me once more with a shutter. "You're a very handsome man . . . you look a bit like Salvador before he gained thirty pounds and went bald . . ."

Great something to look forward to I thought.

"Would you like a taste of my melons . . ."

"What?" I raised an eyebrow a bit afraid I was behind the cage now. I turned around to find a large container of melon, the fruit kind, inches from my face.

"New diet," MaryAnn announced.

Thank God. "Diet . . . but you're perfect," I recovered with a smile.

She laughed with a short high pitched giggle that always reminded me of a hyena. MaryAnn might have been in your face but she was thoroughly skilled at her job when I could persuade her to help me. She was able to find records that had been misplaced thirty years before by simply pausing a moment to think. She gave me an overly familiar squeezing hug that was more groping than Craig's pat down of earlier, before finally asking why I was there.

Several more minutes passed with me being required to taste her melons . . . the ones in the container. Until I finally got the information I'd come about, the Midwest Medical Clinic. I allowed one last departing grope to MaryAnn before leaving. I needed to drop something at home before heading to my meeting.

ഐ

I was going to meet Mr. Zalbowski at his home across the river. Going west as the sun begins to set is never pleasant. The glowing orange orb seemed determined to heat the humid air as much as possible before letting the dark night drop. I was sweating through the sides of my shirt. It was 6:30 and the meeting was for 7:00. The records office had taken me longer than I had anticipated.

The homes were getting smaller as I drove farther away from the richer downtown area. They were moderate average family homes with green lawns filled with children's toys and lawn mowers. I turned down Elm Drive, lined with more locust trees rather than elms. Their tiny fern like leaves rustling in the humid breeze. I still could hardly believe all those enormous elms had died. Something called Dutch Elm disease had wiped them out. I could recall several of the old giants and the thought they had been felled all those years ago . . . I was almost glad I had missed it. One-eighteen, one-twenty, one-twenty two, I counted the house numbers, one-twenty four. There in the middle of the street a single story white house with a double car garage, one-twenty six Elm Drive. I pulled to the curb. A gray SUV was parked in the drive and there was a man out front watering some droopy looking irises.

"Mr. Zalbowski?" I questioned. He swung around turning the hose off just in time not to blast my legs with water, which I appreciated. He wasn't what I had expected, but then not many people were.

"Mr. Taylor?"

"Hello," I said offering my hand. Mr. Zalbowski was a large man with a bit of the look of a bruiser about him. Not exactly how I'd pictured an associate of Joseph's he'd met at the synagogue. The guy was a good inch or two over six foot and from the look of his chest and arms he could probably bench press me without difficulty. Who would be brave enough to take this guy's kid.

"Let's go around back and sit down," Mr. Zalbowski offered with a beefy smile and a reassuring firm hand shake.

I could feel the sweat running down my back as the sun's last rays penetrated my skin. I followed Mr. Zalbowski around his modest house.

Around the back there was a large patio with a metal awning and a small coi pond adjacent. I saw the darting speckled white and orange of a fish disappear into the murky waters depths. Mr. Zalbowski offered me a wooden chair and took a seat himself.

I gazed longingly through the large sliding glass door to the air conditioned comfort of the living room inside. I wiped a bead of sweat from my eyebrow. I guess the hired help didn't get to be refreshed by modern air conditioning.

"I'm glad you came Mr. Taylor," he started looking at me with a concentrated brow that furrowed in a deep crease.

"What can you tell me about Jeffrey, Mr. Zalbowski?"

"He was always a good boy, never even got sick. He had the usual childhood things but . . . I know he would never run away."

"And what makes you say that?" I questioned since he'd already said all this in the staticy message he'd left.

"Because I know my son."

"How old is your son?" I asked wiping away another droplet of sweat.

"He just turned nine in May."

"And when did he go missing?"

"Almost a year ago . . . September seventeenth of last year," he answered.

"Then after school had started."

Mr. Zalbowski nodded.

"That's why you took him to the clinic . . . for school?"

"Yes," he nodded.

"And you were there when they gave him the inoculation?" I asked pulling my shirt away from my skin, where it was beginning to adhere.

"What inoculation? He never got one."

"He never got one?" I questioned with some surprise. It wasn't like Joseph to get something like that wrong.

"No . . . I just need you to find my son . . ." he replied.

"But . . ." I paused. The interior of the house was completely dark and the sun was setting quickly, casting the back patio in dull, dark shadows. "Mr. Zalbowski . . . where's your wife?"

"She's out running errands," he answered.

"So what do you think happened to your son?" I calmly continued making sure I didn't pause as my eyes looked around the patio. Joseph had told me Mr. Zalbowski was a widower, which was what made Jeffrey's disappearance so much worse for him. He didn't respond. "Mr. Zalbowski?" My hand was showing. Oh, crap.

The bruiser's large form moved with greater agility and speed than I expected. He was out of the chair and striking me repeatedly in the face before I raised a hand. Luckily he was big but stupid if that could be lucky. I struck out hard with my right fist into his lower abdomen. The bruiser buckled slightly and stepped back.

"I take it you're not Mr. Zalbowski," I grunted with a half snark.

The bruiser didn't take kindly to my query. He answered me by grabbing a wooden chair and slammed it into my side and back as I rose. I guess smarts didn't matter when you were the size of a wall. I hit the steaming hot cement patio with a scrapping thump of skin on sandpaper. Warm blood, my blood, was dripping from my nose on the gray gritty stone. This meeting was not going well. A kick to the ribs sent me careening into the steps next to the sliding glass door. Crap, my days had to get better. I wheezed and sputtered as needle lightening raced through my nerves screaming as loud as they could that something was wrong. Yelling at me though wasn't helping stop the bruiser's foot from practicing his dancing skills.

A moment's reprieve only signaled he was lifting another large wooden chair above him, but the spear shaped metal legs of the chair grabbed the metal awning above him and stuck. I took the opportunity and launched myself into his ribs. It was stupid. He was built like a wall reinforced with concrete and rebar. I on the other hand was built like a soft side of meat soon to be deboned. He lifted me off the ground by the rib cage and threw me back into the sliding glass door. I hit like a bug on a windshield. My sweat and blood covered skin squeaking down the pane to the sharp cement steps below. He raised the other chair like a pitch fork. This time in both hands ready to run me through with the chairs pointed tong legs. He came at me. With all my might I tried to deflect the legs, my hands pushing them up above me. Good idea, I thought, not getting skewered like a shish kebab. Bad consequence, the legs metal tips struck the sliding glass door with shattering force. My forceful shove had also pushed the bruiser off balance. Now the bruiser brick wall, a bunch of wooden stakes from the chair and shards of sharp glass were all hurdling together with me at the bottom.

The chair's arm caught in the door frame and crashed with splintering cracking force on top of me as the bruiser fell forward on top of the chair. The thick remaining piece of two foot glass at the top of the door dropped, slicing into the bruiser's head. It knocked him out with a deep bloody laceration. Something akin I think to being scalped. I spit, groaning as I raked the jagged wood against my rib cage to get loose from the pile of debris on top of me. Luckily I guess the bruiser had protected me by taking most of the damage from the door.

Scraping away skin and hair until finally I was free; I wiped some blood away from my eyes quickly realizing it hadn't helped since my hands were covered in small cuts from the glass. They were bleeding just as much as my face and neck. But not as much as the unconscious bruiser who'd been scalped. There was a distinct mournful groan from the downed behemoth. He was alive. He didn't look it. But still I looked better than the other guy, so I did what any intelligent person would do. I got the hell out of there. The sun had set and I had no idea if the impersonating felon had friends. I wasn't about to wait and see. I didn't know where the real Mr. Zalbowski was or how they knew I was meeting him. Yes, they because there was no way the unconscious, bleeding brick wall back there was the brains of anything.

I got to my car. Only slipping one foot into the coi pond as I escaped the back yard in a rush, not necessarily a panic, just an intense desire to flee, hoping none of the neighbors had seen me. All I needed was to be stopped by the police, looking like I'd just murdered someone, even though most of the blood was my own. What had I said. There was a neighbor in his driveway with one of those damn phones. I hoped the darkness hid the blood painted across my torso and pants. I got in and drove off never bothering to turn on my headlights, the less description of my car the better. It was painted dark but it wasn't like there were thousands of cars on the streets that looked like my brown beast not any more.

I was across the bridge before my knuckles relaxed on the steering wheel and I started to feel the adrenaline subsiding. I wiped some drying blood away with my shirt. My ribs were aching every small bump in the road now was making them scream. I needed to get home but more I needed to see Joseph. If they knew about me and they knew about Zalbowski . . . they knew about Joseph. I didn't know what had happened to Mr. Zalbowski, even if he was still alive. Or why someone had posed as him and then tried to kill me . . . or at least beat me into near unconsciousness. I had enemies sure, but that had been more than sixty years ago . . . they were all dead . . . and I didn't know anything about this Zalbowski or his son. My concern now was for Joseph, along with a lot of questions about why. Why Jeffrey Zalbowski? What was so important about this kid and his father? Who was after them . . . and now I was somehow involved . . . thanks to Joseph and his good Samaritan ways. I pressed the accelerator a little more and headed for the Rose Tree and Joseph. What had he gotten me into?

Chapter Five

"So then where's Zalbowski?" Joseph questioned handing me a bag of frozen peas for my face, since my nose was nicely swollen by the time I reached the Rose Tree.

"How would I know?" I said holding my head back and pinching the bridge of my nose. There was no way he was going to eat these peas after I was done with them.

We were in his apartment on the top floor of the publishing part of the Rose Tree. I'd scared the bejeezus out of more than one of the employees before Joseph came down and ushered me upstairs. I guess they weren't used to crazed beaten up guys with blood all over them coming in demanding to see their boss. They'd get used to it after they knew me a while. Joseph had just stopped working and was about ready to take a shower, which explained the flapping bath robe.

"Why would they take him? Who are they?" Joseph continued frantically questioning.

"Joseph, sit down," I ordered. His nervous inquiry and open

robe passing by was getting to me. "Zalbowski called me . . . or at least I think he did," I half groaned, rotating the peas to find some that hadn't thawed.

"He did. Didn't he? It was him. Wasn't it?"

"Joseph," I had enough of a headache.

"Sorry," Joseph took a seat for a whole half a second before moving again.

"There was a message on my machine. I assumed it was Zalbowski. Maybe it wasn't."

"But I told him to call . . . he said he'd call," Joseph returned.

"So what's so special about Zalbowski," I questioned laying down the bloody bag of mushy peas on Joseph's kitchen table. The bleeding had stopped and I suddenly realized I'd never been in Joseph's apartment, the third floor of the Rose Tree. It looked like Joseph had crammed it with books and various curiosities, half finished print work and a large television. It was one of those new super flat things. I hadn't seen one of those work. I mean I'd barely even seen televisions in houses so these new thin little things were . . .

"Mel?"

"I don't know," I replied quietly rubbing the tightening muscles in my neck.

"Why don't I call him . . . Zalbowski," Joseph offered.

"He's not home."

"So . . . get into the modern age Mel," Joseph said pulling out a cellular phone from a drawer and flipping through his phone to find Zalbowski's number.

"Trust me I'm in it," I grunted. Joseph passed back and forth. His robe flapping carelessly as he did so from one side of the apartment to the other, revealing more than I cared to see of my friend. "You know that thing will kill you . . ." I said pointing at the phone. I was hurting too much or I would have stepped toward him and made the thing blow up. It was one of the few things my electronic dysfunction was good for.

Joseph ignored me but paced a bit farther away. He knew what I could do. I'd get him to stop using the thing yet.

"Hello . . . Zalbowski . . . this is Joseph, Joseph Morgenstein . . . What . . . ? Where are you?" Joseph motioned to me with a sudden rapid waving. It resembled a wounded chicken more than an attention getter. "What?" Joseph frowned. "You're what . . . being followed."

"Where is he?" I questioned getting up from the chair but making sure I kept my distance from the phone.

"Where are you?" Joseph repeated. "In his car, outside the cities on I-80 . . ." He fell silent listening intently into the phone. "He says they have guns . . . who has guns . . . what . . ."

I didn't waste time and barked orders for Joseph to relay. "Tell him to get someplace crowded quick . . . off the highway . . . now."

"Get someplace crowded, with people, quick," Joseph parroted. "Why?"

"Because if he doesn't you won't be talking to him much longer . . ."

Joseph swallowed. "Because you're in danger . . . yeah . . . good . . . he's pulling into a restaurant now . . ."

"Tell him to go inside . . . to the most crowded part and not move till we get there."

". . . and don't move until we get there . . . Get there!?" Joseph questioned looking back at me, his light blue robe askew.

"Yeah," I returned throwing Joseph a pair of pants from a laundry basket sitting on the floor.

☙❧

We arrived at the Bumblebee's, a chain restaurant, around nine. It had only been an hour since I'd nearly been beaten to a pulp and sliced in half by a sheet of glass. Now I was trying to find a man who was probably a target for assassination or kidnapping or God knows what . . . just like his missing son. The night so far was going well. I had Joseph drive around the parking lot before stopping, hoping I might see something; but spotting would be assassins wasn't as easy as you might think. The parking lot was full of large intimidating vehicles and there were at least a dozen SUVs so we stopped and went inside to locate Zalbowski.

"There he is," Joseph said as we pushed through a crowd of sports fans cheering heartily at the bar. The large liquor bazaar held the center of the restaurant like a giant hollow meeting table or amphitheatre. Alcoholic beverages were the stage actors and the tired workers could appreciate their gladiatorial gods, while drinking sudsy foamed refreshments until their day became an inebriated memory.

Zalbowski was older than I expected. His slightly receding windows peak of curly dark hair was lightly peppered with fine strains of white which from a distance weren't as discernable as up close. His brown eyes were blood shot behind his round wire framed glasses and he was overweight a good thirty or forty pounds for his short stocky frame. He looked exhausted but there was an anxious nervous feel to him. I probably would have looked the same if my son had been kidnapped and I was being chased by people trying to kill me, only I'd look taller.

"Mr. Zalbowski," I said taking a seat in the booth next to him.

He eyed my battered appearance with feared concern, which was relieved somewhat by Joseph's presence, even with the giant grease stain on the front of his pants. It wasn't my fault they were on top of his laundry basket.

"I'm Mel Taylor."

"Taylor . . . you mean the man Joseph told me about . . . ?" his eyes darted to Joseph and then back to me.

"Yes," I started keeping a wary eye on the bustling restaurant and bar. "Can I take it you never called me."

"I did but . . . I was called away to work. I tried to call you but . . ." His speech pattern was stuttered and quick yet the words came out as if they were hard for him to form them in any comprehensive fashion. ". . . your answering machine, it never picked up . . ."

I looked at Joseph who at the moment seemed more nervous than Mr. Zalbowski. His eyes were darting about at every movement in the busy restaurant.

"When I got to the meeting, no one was there . . . they said one had never been called," Zalbowski said running a hand through his short tight curls making them even wilder, which was surprising with his frazzled appearance.

"What time was your meeting?" I questioned.

"Seven," he answered.

I shifted uneasily, we were being played, but by who, and why? They were no doubt still following Mr. Zalbowski. There was probably at least one or two waiting in the parking lot watching Zalbowski's car and one or two watching Zalbowski and us right now. Crap. But there was something I couldn't figure if they took the boy, Jeffrey, almost a year ago, assuming they were the same people. Why would they want Zalbowski now? Why not take him or kill him then? Certainly they had more big bruisers like the one I'd tangled with; it wouldn't have been a problem to find more of the intellectually challenged but muscularly endowed. I'd have to figure it out later, right now there was only one thing I needed to do. I had to get Zalbowski, Joseph, and myself out of here.

"We'll have to leave your car here Mr. Zalbowski," I said. "I'm sure whoever was following you is still keeping an eye on it. Did you see who they were?"

"No . . . not very well. I noticed two men outside work when I went in. Then I noticed them again in the parking lot. Then . . . then a black SUV tried to run me off the road," his words were coming out stuttered and nervous. "I was trying to get away when Joseph called . . . I saw . . . they had guns . . ." His jowly cheeks were flushed.

"I have a feeling these are the same people who took your son."

"Why?" Zalbowski said with a sudden determined voice. His eyes focused at the mention of his son.

"If I knew that Mr. Zalbowski, I'd know a lot more . . ." I returned. Which I give you was not reassuring at all, but what else could I tell him. What was I supposed to tell him . . . the people who had tried to kill you will probably get tired and give up . . . Yeah because that was believable. "Come on gentlemen, we're going to try something. Follow me and stay close together, most importantly keep your eyes open. If they're watching us, they'll follow us."

I edged past the bar, as a rowdy half inebriated cheer erupted at some distant television sports accomplishment. I was glad the TV was far enough away or it might pop out. I made sure to keep my distance as I moved through the center of the restaurant over to the back row of booths, so we were closer to the exit. We had only just sat down when a thin young Bumblebee employee approached us.

"Hello guys," the perky waitress greeted us. She was wearing a striped yellow and black shirt covered in flashy buttons with sayings like 'I'm a worker not a servant,' 'hot mess,' and 'pork for pigs' which I wasn't sure what that last one meant. She stood somewhat motionless for a moment, staring at the three of us before tentatively handing us the menus. "Can . . . can I get you anything . . . ?" she stammered, her eyes still wide.

"You . . ." I said. "Can get us three cokes or whatever," I returned, never bothering to look directly at her face as I said it, which was probably best. I'd forgotten how I looked. I was covered in dried blood, which was luckily turning to a dark brown so it could possibly be mistaken for mud, and my arms and face were battered and covered in tiny cuts. I'm sure as a waitress it wasn't the strangest thing she'd ever seen but it might have been up there with some of them. I could only hope she would ignore it. We didn't need more trouble. I had spied two of the men, no doubt tailing Zalbowski, just off the 'pork for pigs' button on her shoulder. They resembled their colleague whom I had met earlier that evening only they still had their hair, an advantage of not being scalped by a giant piece of thick glass.

"S . . . Sure . . ." she stammered. "Are you ready to, to order . . . or do you . . . need some time?" she asked in startled starts. Hoping we needed a lot more time and she could maybe make a run for it.

"Give us a few minutes," Joseph replied, observing her apprehensive looks far more than I was.

"Okey dokey," she said relieved to be off and turned quickly on her heels.

"Mel, there's two guys at the bar who haven't stopped looking at us since we sat down," Joseph tensed.

"Yeah and there's two more in front of us about six tables away," I replied.

Joseph's eyes grew slightly larger. He hadn't seen them.

"What are we going to do?" Zalbowski questioned pushing his glasses back up onto the bridge of his nose.

It was a good question, now I just needed a good answer. The two at the bar Joseph had spotted were the same size and possessed the same identifying thick unifying brow ridge as my earlier acquaintance. One of these guys had nearly killed me. Four could easily do the job even with Joseph and Mr. Zalbowski to aid me in taking some of their blows.

"Mel?" Joseph's voice was raising with an elevating panic much like his thick hair.

"Give me a minute," I returned. Then a wide smile slowly crossed my lips. "Joseph I could kiss you."

"Now is not the time to make jokes," he grumped at my goofy grin and shook his disgusted head.

"You took me to one of these God awful places last year remember?"

"Yeah. Why? You didn't eat anything," he said frowning and nervously looking around.

"But do you remember what they do for your birthday?" I said with a knowing tone.

"Yeah . . ." Joseph started. "Oh . . ."

"How fast can you guys run?" I looked at the two men across from me with an eager goofy smirk.

"Fast enough," Joseph returned, his feet already pointing away from the table.

"Do you know where the car is from here?"

Joseph looked toward the dark windows, biting his lip. "Yeah, I know," he said a sense of confidence in his voice.

I really hoped it was true. "Mr. Zalbowski get ready," I started.

"For what?" Zalbowski questioned dismayed, his hands twisting a paper napkin into a thin rope.

For my plan I thought.

Our now less than perky waitress had bravely returned with the three cokes. "Are you ready to order?" she asked with an evasiveness that bordered on neglect. I suddenly realized the splatters of drying brown on my shirt were attracting her attention and I don't think she believed it was mud.

"Yes," I returned. "I've got a couple of friends here that are birthday boys," I smiled.

CHAPTER SIX

"Not until I say go gentlemen," I said eyeing the gathering gaggle of employees near the bustling bar.

"Are you sure this will work?" Joseph questioned, his hand gripping the ledge of the table in a position to launch; the tendons in his knuckles raking across the bones with each tightening grasp.

No, but I didn't answer. I just kept my eyes on the forming division of waiters. Suddenly like a well rehearsed military invasion the striped shirts of the employees descended on the two sets of bruisers, just as the call for free drinks went out from the bar. "Now!" I yelled over the chorus of jubilant Happy Birthday. We made it to the exit door but already the bruisers at the bar were wasting no time and pushing through the unprepared waiters. The two at the table were a bit more boxed in and couldn't extract themselves from the merry singing.

"This way!" Joseph cried leading us into the dark parking lot. He had his keys out and ready when he got to the car.

One, there's always one you don't see. There had been one

bruiser in the parking lot. He'd spotted us running from the exit and was headed for us without hesitation. He grabbed for Zalbowski, yanking back on the collar of his jacket and shirt with a sudden chocking gag. But he didn't see me, and I clocked him with a jabbing elbow to the eye socket. The man dropped his grip on Zalbowski's collar and grabbed his face with a whimpering moan. Zalbowski coughed and sputtered but he was free.

"Go Joseph! Go!" I yelled slamming the door and making sure Zalbowski was in the back seat. Joseph gunned his sedan over the grass divider in reverse. The sound of metal grating against cement was deafening. If anything was destroyed we'd find out later, what mattered was the car was still moving. Joseph hadn't bothered to put the car in forward until we were on the road, amongst blaring car horns and skidding brakes. "Joseph!"

"I'm going," he barked shoving the gear into drive. We started forward just as two of the bruisers emerged from the restaurant.

Joseph sped off down the road, pushing the car as hard as his foot would go against the accelerator. The engine was struggling to commit to the demand. Something metal was scoring the pavement but not for long as it tore loose from the under carriage with a crashing sound amongst the traffic. Cars swerved behind us. The crunching twist of metal and plastic striking each other as the traffic lanes behind us ground to a colliding halt with a chorus of horns and yells.

"This is the second car you've destroyed," Joseph growled a wild look in his eyes as we raced along the highway.

"*You* insisted on driving . . . and *you're* the one that backed over the divider," I turned scanning the road behind us. I saw nothing but a traffic jam and gridlock. "Take the first exit. The sooner we get into town the better," I said.

Joseph complied, turning off a few seconds later.

I turned from the rear window and Mr. Zalbowski. Who looked about as shaken and pale as when we'd first entered the restaurant. "Let's hope they don't follow us."

"But they know where you live, where I live . . . don't they? Will we be safe at your place?" Joseph questioned.

"I'd feel safer there than somewhere else," I replied rubbing my ribs. Joseph may have been right; but they didn't want us. They wanted Zalbowski . . . and now we had him. I just had to figure out why they wanted him and who they were and about half a dozen other things. This had not been a good day or a little favor.

 exo

Joseph cautiously rolled the wheels of his shaking sedan onto the gravel drive by my house, next to my old brown beast.

"Pull around back, next to the trees," I told him.

The car was rattling but running.

Joseph pulled to a stop. The headlights were already off. I had him switch them off when we came down the street. He shut the engine off with a sputter and the three of us remained silent and still in the darkness of the car. There was barely a breath of air in the maple trees next to us.

"What time do you think it is?" Joseph questioned with a whisper.

"12:34," I answered without hesitation.

"How do you know that?"

"Because it always is," I returned with a pale sigh. "I didn't see any other cars on the street. Even Mr. Delmar's lights are off," I quickly added. Mr. Delmar was my nearest neighbor and my nosiest. His house was on the other side of my gravel driveway. I'd forced Joseph to drive his rattling sedan around for more than an hour just to make sure no one was following us before we made any attempt to stop. No black SUVs or little blue Volkswagen beetles . . . thank God. My ear was still hurting even over the cuts and scraps from the bruiser.

"Do you think there's anyone out there," Zalbowski quietly asked from the back seat.

I stared up at my old brick building. I sure hoped not. My ribs were killing me from the tense last few hours and the speeding bumpy car escape. "Come on," I opened the car door slowly. Joseph and Mr. Zalbowski did the same. I was just closing mine with a soft click when Joseph slammed his shut.

"Oh sorry," he whispered with a cringe.

"Little late for that now," I scolded and waved for the two men to follow me. The slammed door hadn't alerted anyone that I could see, but my lack of observance didn't reassure me. I pulled my keys out of my pocket. Feeling the framing of the heavy metal back door, I felt for the key hole with my fingertips.

A moment later and we were all safely inside my brick house behind locked doors. I left Joseph and Mr. Zalbowski in the kitchen and went all the way to the front of my building and my office. Looking through the front glass to the dark street, I couldn't see anyone. There were no cars, no blue Volkswagens. I turned back glancing at my desk filled with papers and files. Something was missing. I hadn't seen it before, my new answering machine, no wonder Zalbowski couldn't leave a message. That was how they knew he had called me. How they knew when the meeting was. Now just who were they. The blue Volkswagen, the early morning break in; whoever it had been had stolen my answering machine. Crap that one had worked. It must have been the same people chasing us tonight. But why? I unscrewed the receiver of my dial phone. If they were listening in it was on Zalbowski's line, not mine. There weren't many listening devices that would have even half worked around me. Most devices would have just caught my phone on fire with me using it . . . like I said it wasn't just light bulbs I fried. I hung up the phone and headed back to the kitchen, making sure the thick curtains that separated my office from the rest of my house were securely shut. The curtains weren't just for privacy and light. They made sure we were safe from other possibilities.

"Well, were we followed?" Joseph questioned on my return, his hair somehow still defying gravity even at this hour.

"I didn't see anyone," I said. Joseph had given Zalbowski a bottle of my mead, while he was holding a glass of water and some sort of rapidly made sandwich. He'd apparently scavenged from the contents of my fridge.

"Not that we all don't, but you look like crap man," Joseph said taking a bite of his sandwich.

"Yeah well I feel like it too," I looked at my arms. They were covered in small dried cuts and smears of hastily wiped away blood. I was surprised I hadn't gotten more stares at the restaurant. Maybe it was a good thing I had given Joseph the soiled pants with the giant stain of grease.

"Let me go wash myself up a bit then we can regroup."

"Sure," Joseph said opening the fridge again. His sandwich was already gone. Mr. Zalbowski was silent staring at the brown bottle as though it was a condensating crystal ball.

෨ඁ෬

When I finally looked in the mirror of my little bathroom I realized Joseph had made an understatement. My nose and left eye were severally swollen. My short sleeved light blue shirt was covered in smears and drops of muddied, dried blood, probably half mine and half the other guys. I unbuttoned the shirt to reveal long jagged raking marks across my rib cage and upper chest. The outer skin had been torn away leaving welted lines intensely dotted by blood beneath the surface of my remaining flesh. I opened the cabinet and pulled out a small brown jar. I was covered in slowly developing bruises and nearly every motion pulled at something that didn't want to move. I pulled another tall blue bottle from the cabinet as well.

I jumped, or rather gingerly stepped, into the shower first. The water was cold because I hadn't heated enough ahead of time, so it was freezing. My muscles contracted in uncontrollable sudden jerks but I'd survive. It was cold but filtered. See I have a real problem dosing myself in the same chemicals I'd seen used to kill people during the war . . . that's World War II . . . thus the filtered water. I jittered and sloshed water in a rapid attempt and deluded theory that if you moved more you'd stay warm while taking a cold shower, it doesn't work. Once I was clean and dry, I picked up the brown jar. The yellow green salve burned slightly on the open scratches as

I spread it across the long racked marks. I wiped my fingers off and unscrewed the top of the blue bottle. I took one long deep swig. It didn't have much of a taste and I was thankful I had to drink it and not the yellow green salve that was already wafting up to my nostrils with its pungent odor. There was a reason I grew those plants in the basement besides their austere beauty. I pushed my hair back and grabbed a black t-shirt. The salve wouldn't show or stain.

ळ

By the time I returned Joseph had stopped eating me out of house and home. How he stayed so slim I didn't know. Mr. Zalbowski had almost finished his mead and I looked half way respectable.

I grabbed a large glass and filled it up with water.

"That's a puny little faucet you have there," Joseph injected.

"That's cause it's not a faucet to the main water. It's to my filter tanks."

"Filter tanks?" Joseph questioned still with enough energy to be curious. He'd only been in my house a few times and usually in the office or living room.

"Reverse osmosis," I replied. "Remind me to tell you about the poisons in the water," I drank nearly the whole glass at once. I think Joseph was still too stunned by the night's events to want to know exactly what I meant. "Now Mr. Zalbowski, do you have any idea who those men were? Or what they want?"

"No," he replied. "I haven't got a clue." It was obvious that for the last hour or so he'd been pondering that very question. "I don't have anything. I'm not rich. I'm not important. My job isn't special.

67

I sell art supplies . . . you know to artists . . . it's just me and Jeffrey and now . . . I . . . I just don't understand . . ."

I rubbed my face. The small cuts were pulling as they dried and sealed after the shower. I didn't get it either. There had to be a reason for Jeffrey's disappearance and the attack on his father now almost a year later. But what was it.

"The only thing I can hope is that Jeffrey's still alive . . ." he sighed in a deep exhale. Hope I think was the only thing still sustaining the poor guy. I wasn't about to dissuade him. Hope was all the man had left, even if hope was as battered and cut as I was.

Joseph patted Zalbowski on the shoulder. "God will help," Joseph said quietly.

Mr. Zalbowski bowed his head.

I'm sure he would but in one of those more mysterious ways instead of something really practical or helpful like a post card explaining everything or Jeffrey just showing up at my back door. I sat down and drank the rest on my water then leaned forward. "Mr. Zalbowski," I started my eyes focused on him and his sagging defeated appearance. "I need you to tell me everything you can remember about Jeffrey's disappearance."

Mr. Zalbowski took a long, deep breath, looked me in the eye with his large brown puppy dog eyes, that seemed even sadder and more blood shot through his round wire frames, and started. "He was going to start third grade. The school required a medical examine. They gave me the name of the medical clinic . . . they said the clinic had done examines for nearly all the children." It was to the point and simple, more it was obvious he had repeated the same facts hundreds of times to police officers, detectives, investigators and just about anyone who would listen or possibly help.

"The school did?" I asked.

"Yes, they said they had been using them for years. So I took Jeffrey a week before school started. It was a routine examine . . . only," Mr. Zalbowski stopped. "They said the school required a booster shot on one of Jeffrey's vaccinations. They assured me it was normal . . . for all the children entering the third grade," his eyes fluttered but he held his own. The poor guy had I'm sure inflicted enough guilt on himself over the long months since his son had gone missing. He'd blamed himself for everything even the things not in his control. I know I'd have done the same thing.

I wasn't about to inflict what I knew about the vaccination programs on Mr. Zalbowski. He already had enough on his plate but I couldn't help the slight grimaces that came across my face when he mentioned them.

"Do you think I was wrong? Did I do something to my son?" his voice filled with anguish. "I knew I shouldn't have . . ." his hand pushed his glasses up then rubbed across his lips and the shadow of beard that was beginning to appear.

"Please Mr. Zalbowski just tell me what happened next," I tried to focus him.

He took a stuttered breath and continued. "He was fine the first couple of days, normal, loving, happy, active kid . . ." Zalbowski paused, the memory lighting a small smile on his lips. "Then he said he didn't feel well. He ran a slight fever . . . but the next day he was better . . . and by Monday and the start of school he seemed fine," Zalbowski paused again. "I took him to school Tuesday morning

like normal. He seemed fine . . . healthy, happy. I don't remember
seeing anyone, you know watching or lurking about . . . as a parent
you always look for those things. I watched him go into the school.
He waved goodbye . . . ." Zalbowski held his hand to his mouth,
attempting to steady his next words before speaking. The last image
of his son now etched in his memory. "They had recess after lunch.
I got a call around 1:30 . . . the teachers couldn't find Jeffrey. They
said he must have wandered off . . . he didn't . . . . Jeffrey's a smart
boy. He wouldn't go off with someone, anyone, and he wouldn't just
leave school . . . not without calling me. If he wanted to leave I would
have come and gotten him. I would have gotten him . . ."

"And the police?" I questioned.

"The file . . . it's in my car . . ." his eyes widened, his car which
we had left behind at the restaurant.

"It doesn't matter Mr. Zalbowski . . ." I waved off his concern.
". . . just tell me what you remember . . ." The police had given up
so I doubted his copy of their report would shed any new light on
what they already didn't know.

"There was one camera . . . that showed Jeffrey walking in
the parking lot . . . I know my son Mr. Taylor . . ." his soft brown
eyes looked at me. "He did not run away." On this one fact Mr.
Zalbowski was emphatic.

"I believe you Mr. Zalbowski. If anything, tonight alone proves
something is not as it seems."

"The police said he ran away," Zalbowski's words were etched
with sorrow. "There was no evidence someone took him. No
witnesses, no strange vehicles, nothing . . . when they couldn't find
anything . . . it was almost as if they didn't care, the police . . . ."

after a while . . . I put up posters. I searched fields, streets, went door to door."

I could see the events, each hope and disappointment playing out in the man's mind before me.

"I hired an investigator . . . well actually two. The first one . . . he wouldn't take the job. The second one stayed at it for two weeks before . . . well he just said there was nothing to go on and the police were probably right . . . Jeffrey had run away . . . it was just like he disappeared off the face of the planet."

"No one disappears completely Mr. Zalbowski, no one," I replied. Even I hadn't, I'd just gotten shucked to another time.

"I just want my son back. I just want someone to believe me," he grimaced in an expression of pain.

"We believe you Mr. Zalbowski."

"Yeah," Joseph added. "We believe you."

Mr. Zalbowski took several deep breaths and rubbed his tired features.

"It's two in the morning gentlemen," I said pulling out my silver pocket watch and giving it a thorough nightly wind. There wasn't much more we could do tonight. I felt we were as secure in my old brick house as we would be anywhere more than anything we all needed rest. I knew I did. My body was aching and tired from being beaten and chased. "I suggest we try to get some rest; perhaps clearer minds will prevail." They were both too tired and numb to protest. Each gave me a nod of agreement.

I offered my bed to Mr. Zalbowski, while Joseph and I headed for the living room. Joseph took the sofa since he was short enough to lie down on it, while I took one of the more comfortable worn leather chairs pulling over the green cushioned foot stool. Thoughts and questions ran through my mind without pause but at least the salve was starting to work and soon the exhaustion of the day and the late hour overwhelmed my senses. I slipped into the quiet pleasure of sleep, sometimes I really did.

CHAPTER SEVEN

It was my stomach that woke me with a growling churning anger. I hadn't eaten since late afternoon yesterday. I sat forward slowly, the bruises on my back were yelling, more they were seriously pissed I had slept in a chair all night. Joseph was still asleep, one leg on and one leg off the sofa. I had to say the giant grease stain on his pants looked awful. It was dark brownish black and slightly shiny. It ran half way down his right leg from the belt buckle and crotch area.

"Joseph," I said smacking him in the head with a pillow. His shock of thick dark hair was usually pointed up in the front but now it was accompanied by the rest of his hair jabbing out in every conceivable way, along with a good growth of stubbly beard covering his cheeks and chin.

"Wha . . ." Joseph groaned as the pillow thapped him and he fell off the sofa.

"Joseph."

"Oh right," he said still dazed, scratching his cheek as he sat up on the floor.

"Go check on Zalbowski. I'll make some breakfast."

"Breakfast," Joseph said perking up almost immediately. "Zalbowski . . . right, right on my way," he groaned rising from the floor and shuffled down the hall to my bedroom in his stocking feet.

My protective curtains were still drawn so I pulled my watch out to check the time. It was nearly seven in the morning. I gave my silver pocket watch its morning wind and fought gravity with each step to the kitchen. About thirty minutes later we were scarfing down our eggs and oatmeal cakes, fresh from the skillet. Luckily I had leftover oatmeal in the fridge, which Joseph hadn't eaten.

☯

"So Mel, what's with the curtains?" Joseph said putting his fork down, his plate empty before the rest of us. "They're heavy as hell."

"That's because they're bulletproof."

Joseph half chuckled. "Seriously," he returned skeptically.

"They also purify the air, block electromagnetics . . . and they look nice."

Joseph laughed.

"I'm not kidding." I returned completely sober.

"Where do you get something like that?" he questioned with a disbelieving scoff, his eyebrows frowning. "And more importantly why do you need something like that . . . bulletproof . . . what afraid of drive-bys?"

"You don't get them. You make them and well . . . it's best to be ready."

"Yeah but ready for what?" Joseph returned with a raised

eyebrow reexamining my curtains, I think for the first time a bit more concerned about what I did in my spare time. Maybe also realizing he really didn't know all that much about me.

ॐ

We waited until Mr. Zalbowski had returned to my bedroom to freshen up before saying anything. But I knew Joseph was sitting on a question. He had been since about half way through breakfast.

"Are you going to tell him?" Joseph questioned once Zalbowski had left the room.

"Tell him what?" I returned, still sitting at my small wooden kitchen table across from Joseph.

"The thousands of possibilities of what happened to his son . . . and which one is probably true . . ."

"What do you think happened?" I returned, perhaps not yet willing to let my mind wander to the darker possibilities just yet.

Joseph took a quick look to make sure Zalbowski was still behind closed doors or at least down the short hall in my bedroom. "I think something went wrong and some rogue doctor or pharmaceutical giant is cleaning up the loose ends," he offered with a pointed look.

"Cynical . . . and probably a good guess . . . but that doesn't make sense. Zalbowski says Jeffrey wasn't even sick. Second, why wait a year to go after the father when even the police don't care about the case. Heck, when it appears nobody's interested in the case. Why go after the father at all, if the kid was the important one. No . . ." I shook my head. "There's way more to this. We just don't know what it is," I paused.

"Do you think we should call the police?" Joseph asked.

"They didn't help him before . . ."

"But now, I mean . . . they or somebody tried to kill him and us . . . and you . . ."

"No I don't think the police are the next best step . . ."

"Then what?" Joseph questioned.

"How well do you know Zalbowski?" I asked raising a suspicious eyebrow. I didn't like where my pessimistic thoughts were now taking me but it was a valid avenue I hadn't gone down, probably because I hadn't wanted to go down it.

"Not really well . . . why?" Joseph questioned with some skepticism.

"Did he ask you for help . . . or . . ."

"No . . . if you're thinking he might have had something to do with his own son's . . ." Joseph looked at me aghast. "No my mother told me about him. He'd only just started coming to the synagogue . . . he'd never . . ."

"Ok, ok . . . I just . . . it doesn't make sense. Why wait a year . . . I mean the police had given up . . ." I suddenly had a clear thought. "Why . . . maybe because whoever . . . *they* are found out he'd hired someone new . . ."

"What . . . like maybe they're afraid of genealogists," Joseph half chuckled.

I doubted that very much, no there had to be something else I was missing or maybe I was just paranoid. But paranoia had served me well in the past . . . and when I say past . . . I mean *past*.

Joseph gave me a strained look.

"What?" I questioned.

"Do we really think his . . . that Jeffrey is still alive."

I didn't answer right away, that was enough of an answer I think for Joseph. He dropped his hands to the table and lowered his head. We both had the same thought . . . the kid was probably already dead.

"I know my son is alive," Zalbowski was standing in the open doorway that led to my bedroom. "And I didn't have anything to do with his disappearance."

"I never thought you had Mr. Zalbowski," I returned. I hadn't really but I had to ask.

"He's alive," he insisted with a stern determined look that somehow rose above his downtrodden short appearance.

"He could be," Joseph started. "But you need to be prepared . . . that's all we're saying . . ."

"I'll mourn him when it's time to mourn not before . . ." Zalbowski said with the first aggressive tone I'd heard from the man. He pushed his round wire rimmed glasses back up to the bridge of his nose and stared at Joseph with tired determination. He had been fighting for so long he wasn't prepared to stop, not yet and by the look I now saw in his eyes, maybe never.

"Ok, ok," I said before things escalated. We had slept but we were all still tired. We were all starting to fray a bit especially Zalbowski.

The sudden jangle of the front bell jolted us all back into reality.

"See who it is," I said to Joseph. Who quickly stepped through the living room and stuck his head through the drawn curtains.

"It's a woman," he returned with surprise. "A pretty woman, with dark hair . . . do you know her?" Joseph questioned with profound skepticism.

"Oh God, it's Miss Haptonstall," I had completely forgotten.

"Haptonstahl? Is that Jewish?"

"It's English. Go let her in, before anyone sees her," I grunted.

Joseph hurried through the curtains, running his fingers through his unruly jutting hair.

I guess there was now an even better reason for letting her work at home. Her first day, I had been robbed. The second day her boss looked like he'd gone ten rounds with a heavy weight. God only knew what day three would bring.

Joseph pulled the curtains securely tight once again after escorting her inside and into the living room. I noted her lack of concern at Joseph's action. She didn't bat an eye, unlike when I had locked my front door the day before. Emily looked around the room. There was her battered boss, a rumpled, exhausted overweight man, who looked like he was on the run, which he was, and Joseph, who was smiling inappropriately and trying to appear nonchalant in his stained pants and badly combed sofa hair.

"Miss Haptonstall, we have to reschedule," I started.

"Is it like this around here all the time?" she questioned.

You had to say those Haptonstall's were a hardy stock. "Not all the time," I replied.

"Just most of the time," Joseph returned and quickly grew silent as I glared at him.

"Actually I need you to do something for me," I said with a second thought. "Look him up, Isaac Zalbowski," I pointed to Mr. Zalbowski.

Zalbowski's tired features didn't even rise.

"Look him up?" Emily questioned with a raised eyebrow. "What do you mean look him up?" her voice even and polite.

"On that computer thing . . ." I clarified.

She frowned.

"The internet," Joseph tried to clear up my words.

"What? Now? You want me to go home and look him up now . . . and do what?" she asked holding up her hands expecting a better explanation than probably any I could give her. Which . . . I probably could have given her one, but if she was going to work for me she was going to have to get used to odd requests and garbled instructions. Joseph should have put that in the flyer.

"She doesn't have to go home. She can come to my place," Joseph offered. He sincerely meant it, but somehow it came out more like a bad pick up line than intended.

"I'm afraid I don't understand," Emily began a bit defensive. I don't think she was offended by Joseph. She just ignored his less than flattering proposal and gave me a questioning focused stare. "What am I looking for?"

"That's a better idea Joseph," I returned, understanding Joseph's words.

"It is." They both returned.

"But we'll use the back door again, just in case," I said.

"In case of what?" Emily questioned as we all started moving. "And go where?" No doubt beginning to wonder what type of job she had taken and whether all of those present were more than a little . . . well crazy.

"Come along Mr. Zalbowski." The man was tired and frazzled and I couldn't blame him. He'd already had almost a year of worry and now people were trying to kill him. I could relate. Things like this tended to get a lot worse before they got better . . . if they ever got better. I mean I was still waiting to see on my own situation.

"Where are *we* going?" Emily repeated having not moved from her firmly held spot by the curtains. I could have made a Wizard of Oz reference about discovering what was behind the curtain but I didn't. There was no need to add more confusion to an already bewildering situation.

"To Joseph's to use one of those internet devices," I returned.

"You don't have a computer?" she questioned, sounding slightly astonished.

"It's a long story," Joseph replied helping Mr. Zalbowski.

"Don't worry I have my phone," Emily said pulling it out.

"It won't work in here," I began as she frustratedly hit buttons. "Not with the curtains drawn."

"What's wrong with this thing?"

"Come on," I said grabbing her arm. Why did everybody use those blasted things.

Joseph was about to offer his advice that she just go outside the curtains, but he knew better.

"Put that thing away," I grunted at her phone, as I pulled her toward my kitchen. Her phone began beeping then made a noise I don't think it was supposed to, because Emily flinched before throwing it back in her bag with disgust.

"Wait," she pulled her arm free of my hold. "Not until you explain . . ."

"Ah . . ." I stopped, looking at her now steely blue eyes that had narrowed with some resistance.

"Really he doesn't mean to be an ass. He just is . . ." Joseph started. ". . . but we could use your help . . . especially Mel . . ."

Emily's features softened slightly.

"What he said," I offered with my best smile.

Emily took a long moment, glanced from me to Joseph to Mr. Zalbowski and finally back to me. I could see her mind reasoning out the situation. We didn't look dangerous, so much as beaten, tired, dirty and a little pathetic. "Fine . . ." she sighed. She couldn't believe she was doing this . . . she couldn't believe *why* she was doing this . . .

I smiled with triumph. I could always count on a Haptonstall. All four of us exited my brick building through the back door.

"Well let's see if it will run," Joseph said jingling his keys and we all got in Joseph's car. Emily and Zalbowski got in the back, Joseph and myself in the front. I said a little silent prayer hoping I hadn't destroyed Joseph's car completely. It made a horrendous whining sound similar to a cat being skinned alive but the engine caught and hosanna, it went forward. I made a feeble attempt to explain who Mr. Zalbowski was to Emily and why we were headed to Joseph's. It was feeble and she knew it. We had railroaded her into our little adventure for ten dollars an hour.

☙❧

"It's over there," Joseph said pointing to the flat screen and computer tower across the room in his upstairs apartment. Emily headed for it immediately, trying not to trip on the numerous items scattered about Joseph's floors, mostly clothes and books; happy I think to have something on which to focus beyond my crazy abnormalcy. I began guiding Mr. Zalbowski after her.

"Wait!" Joseph said jumping in front of us. "That's my business computer. I have business files on there. You know the things I make a living at. I've seen what you do to lights. Stay in my kitchen." It was the most aggressive and forceful tone I'd ever heard from Joseph. I could understand now how he ran three different businesses.

"Alright," I shrugged and led Mr. Zalbowski back out to the kitchen, with its bright yellow walls and linoleum counters.

"Ok, what do I . . ." Emily turned around to find me pacing back and forth in the kitchen at the far other end of the apartment; as Joseph and his stained pants stood beside her. "What, are we going to yell across the apartment?"

"Something like that," I yelled from the kitchen.

"Mr. Morgenstein?" an older heavy set woman opened Joseph's apartment door with a knock.

"Mrs. Robinson," Joseph said nearly tripping over a low table as he quickly made his way back across the apartment.

"I just had a question on the city printing order." I could see her perfectly permed fake blonde head swiveling about the various characters in the room. Her eyes were now closely examining my bruised features. I smiled which didn't seem to comfort her.

"Yes, Mrs. Robinson," Joseph said closing his door and momentarily pushing her out into the hall. "Don't go near the computer," he pointed a stern finger at me.

I put up a hand of surrender. It wasn't like I had destroyed his computer before, just his truck . . . and now maybe his car. The chances of the computer catching fire or exploding were pretty small at most it would probably just go goofy or . . .

"What do you want me to look up?" I heard Emily question from the other room.

I turned to Mr. Zalbowski. He had a dazed far off look in his blood shot eyes tinged by the hope that everything over the last few hours and perhaps year had been a horrible nightmare. "Mr. Zalbowski? Is there anything special about Jeffrey?"

His brown eyes stared up at me through the wire rimmed frames, the lenses of his glasses giving them an even more forlorn puppy appearance. "Everything about Jeffrey is special," he answered.

"I know that . . ." I returned softly. ". . . but anything . . . physically special when he was born . . . or . . ."

"His mother died in childbirth . . . but that isn't special . . ." his face somehow growing even more forlorn.

"What about your wife or you Mr. Zalbowski . . . anything unusual . . . ?"

He shook his head.

"Your wife's parents, your parents?"

He shrugged and shook his head. "My father was a Holocaust survivor . . ."

"He was?"

Mr. Zalbowski nodded.

"Did you hear that?" I questioned Emily.

"Need a name?" she replied. Her back still turned, facing the computer, so the only thing I could see was her dark auburn hair and straight shoulders.

"Moshe . . . Moshe Zalbowski," Mr. Zalbowski replied, taking in a sudden breath. "But what does that have to do with Jeffrey?"

"I hope nothing," I returned.

I heard the keys clicking on the computer and took two steps toward the other room. I looked back at the door. Joseph still hadn't returned. I continued asking Mr. Zalbowski questions and relaying them to Emily as I took a few more cautious steps. "He was born in 1919 in Poland . . ." I said.

"Shouldn't you be in the kitchen," Emily said with a slightly authoritative question.

"A Polish Jew . . . in Auschwitz . . ."

"I heard him, unfortunately it's not a small number," she returned with a solemn tone. "This will take some time . . ."

"Right," I returned and paced back to the kitchen, where Mr. Zalbowski was now cradling his head at the small kitchen table. I pushed the sudden horrifying memories from my own mind and tried to focus on the cheesy yellow walls that were the color of sunshine. I didn't want to relive what I had seen or what I remembered.

Several minutes passed as Emily clicked away at the computer, her form concentrated and silent. "Got it," Emily called as Joseph returned to the apartment.

"What? What did you find?" Joseph asked.

"What?" I half yelled over Joseph's question.

"He was transferred to Auschwitz in . . . 1944, Moshe Zalbowski. He was apparently selected for experiments by Nazi doctors at the camp. One of the few survivors . . ."

Mr. Zalbowski shuddered, never raising his head.

"What doctors?" I questioned. The hairs at the back of my neck sticking out like warning antennas. I waited as Emily took several more long minutes of clicking and typing.

"Dr. Mengele . . ." she started reading off the list of infamous names most of which I was unfortunately familiar with, nothing struck a cord until she reached the last name. ". . . and Dr. Ernst . . ."

"Ernst!?" my body suddenly lost all feeling. The memories I had been trying to avoid flooded my senses with all the subtly of a freight train. I landed in the other small table chair across from Mr. Zalbowski, the metal casters of the chair scrapping across the worn linoleum floor.

"Yes, Dr. D. Ernst," Emily innocently replied. "Why?"

"Crap," I groaned. "That's why they took him."

CHAPTER EIGHT

"What? What are you talking about?" Joseph stammered. "You think Nazis have him. That Nazis are after us?" he sat down hard on the sofa never bothering to move the print proofs, that he'd now crushed. "You mean those bald angry white guys, right? Neo Nazis?" he questioned with surprising hope in his voice.

"No I don't mean Neo Nazis," I returned. "I need to get back to my house."

"Your house, why?" Joseph questioned.

"Because I might know who has Jeffrey."

"Who?" Mr. Zalbowski was up and alert at the mention of his son.

I don't think he was alert so much about the mention of Nazis, because let's face it who wants to hear that. But alert at the more important thing, that there might now be some clue to finding his son.

"You don't want to know," I returned.

"I do," his eyes were intense, still blood shot, but suddenly focused.

"Trust me you don't. Or you'll wish your son was dead."

The hope that had dawned in Mr. Zalbowski's soft brown eyes faded.

"Take him down to the car, will you Joseph?"

Joseph reluctantly nodded. He led Zalbowski out of the apartment and started down the stairs.

"How could you say that to him?" Emily questioned with a scolding tone crossing the room from the computer.

"Because the kid would be better off dead, if he's with the type of people I think he might be with," I returned. "Thank you Miss Haptonstall, you did very good for your first day," I turned toward the door.

"Wait a minute," she said following me. "Is that it?"

"Yes, part time remember. Unless you want to work for free," I gave her an enthusiastic glance.

Her blue eyes glared at me with steely disapproval. She was shorter than I was but her look intimidated me. "It hasn't been a full hour."

"I'll pay you ten dollars anyway."

"Then you get a full hour," she replied.

I couldn't help but smile sarcastically at that, come on I was being polite just letting that one slip by.

"Oh stop," she said and opened the door. "Or I'll sue you for sexual harassment and get a lot more than ten dollars."

My smile quickly faded.

ℰ𝒳𝒪

"What took you so long," Joseph grumped from the front seat of his rattling but amazingly still running sedan.

"Nothing," I returned as Emily got in the back seat with Mr. Zalbowski.

"*Sure*," he said intimating something.

"Just drive," I grunted. It only took a few seconds to drive from the Rose Tree to my house; but I kept my eyes open observing any cars that passed us. "Whoa! Slow down, park here Joseph."

"What? Why?" he questioned slowing down and starting to pull over on the far end of the street.

"Blue Volkswagen."

"Seriously . . . Nazis drive a blue Volkswagen?" Joseph scoffed, but pulled to the curb.

"They invented them," I added.

Joseph gulped. "Now what do we do?" he asked scratching his stubbled cheek as he kept his eyes focused on the little cerulean beetle in the distance.

"I need to get into my house."

"Honestly," Emily sputtered from the back seat, pulling her phone out and quickly dialing.

"Hey," I started to protest, amazed the thing still even worked as close as she was to me.

"Yes, I need a police car . . ." she leaned away from me in the front seat instinctively realizing I was the main issue with her phone not working. "Yes . . . to check something out . . . My grandmother lives on eighteenth street and there's been a blue Volkswagen out front for the past several hours. I think they may be selling drugs or something. People keep coming up to the car and driving away . . . . Yes ma'am, . . . I would appreciate that . . . my name . . . Mary Delmar."

I was impressed and more than a little frightened by the relative easy at which she lied. More I was reminded of another young woman with the same last name, Haptonstall, who thought just as well on her feet.

"Give it a couple of minutes," Emily said hanging up her phone . . . or tried to since it made a rather strange beeping sound that caused her to frown at it. I didn't say a word I told her not to use it. It wasn't my fault if it never worked again . . . ok maybe it was my fault, but I didn't feel all that bad about it.

"Definitely worth ten dollars an hour," Joseph smiled, not bothering to look across at me.

She was right less than fifteen minutes later a squad car pulled up along side the blue Volkswagen. There was an exchange of words with the unseen driver and the Volkswagen began to pull away from the curb.

"Ok, I'm impressed," I admitted it. I was. "Everybody duck," I said realizing the blue bug was going to pass right by us. I figured Joseph's car was obvious enough without four people sitting there waving at whoever was about to pass.

"Seriously?" Emily questioned, but we all leaned down below the windows.

It might have seemed silly to duck down like a bunch of kids but what were we supposed to do, wave. "Now let's just hope they were the only look out," I said gesturing to Joseph to start the car.

Joseph's sedan pulled once again into my gravel drive and around my brown beast and Emily's car, toward the back of the building. My neighbor Mr. Delmar was sitting on his porch craning his neck to watch the unfamiliar and noisy rattling car pull around my building, letting out three strange people and me. Of course to Mr. Delmar he probably counted me as one of the strange people, so it was four.

"How did you know my neighbor's name was Delmar?" I questioned Emily as I unlocked the steel back door to my house.

"It's on the mailbox," she said strolling inside.

"So much for observant," Joseph said.

"Shut up," I returned pushing him inside.

"So we're back again," Mr. Zalbowski sighed. "What does my father or any of this have to do with my son?"

"That's what I hope to find out," I said locking the back door and leading them from the kitchen into the living room to the round circular iron staircase that led up to the second story.

The three followed me, Mr. Zalbowski, Emily and Joseph bringing up the rear. We exited the staircase onto the second floor entering a rather small unimpressive room, that contained a reading chair, floor lamp and a large wooden chest that all sat on top of a worn Persian area rug. Perhaps the most unique item was an old gramophone on a stand with a large number of records held beneath. My three guests were obviously not impressed nor did I expect them to be. Where I was headed lay beyond one of the three doors in the small room. I stepped toward the door several yards in front of me.

I removed a key from my pocket and proceeded to unlock the wooden door.

"You keep a room in your own house locked?" Joseph questioned raising an eyebrow.

"Please," I said ushering them in the dark open rectangle.

"Mel . . . how about some light . . ." Joseph muttered. "I can't see a thing . . ."

I proceeded behind them, switching on the light only after I had closed the door to the outer room and stairs.

ೞೞ

They had definitely not expected the immensity of the room with its high twenty foot ceilings. The room occupied nearly the entire top floor of my old brick building. I crossed the room pulling back the curtains from the three narrow, long windows to flood the room with day light, revealing more of their shocked expressions.

"Good God," Joseph exclaimed zeroing in almost immediately on the long fifty foot wall of floor to ceiling book shelves crammed with various tomes and titles.

I didn't waste time and headed for a group of ten wooden filing cabinets on the other wall. I looked over to Mr. Zalbowski and Miss Haptonstall, who were still standing a bit slack jawed at the chasm like room. The high old ceiling with its copper colored tin impressed designs only added to the overwhelming impression of my little extra curricular activities. I was revealing a layer of myself no other person knew and for a very long time I thought no one would ever know. It was a side of me that would probably raise more questions than I cared to share, but this wasn't about me. This was a about a boy. I could live with anything if it meant saving his life.

I watched Miss Haptonstall's eyes traveling along the various surfaces, to the book shelves, paperwork, tables, cases, trunks, typewriter and equipment until she came to my giant board. It was a large cork board covered in a map with names and flagged locations indicated in red and blue colors. Her eyes narrowed. Her smooth brow furrowed. I wasn't sure what she would make of it.

I found what I was looking for and pulled the file from the cabinet, slapping it with more than needed sound onto my large circular table in the center of the room. "This is what I needed. Joseph if you can pull yourself away I need that file on the card catalog."

But Joseph's head was twisted to one side intent on reading the spines of my books. It was Miss Haptonstall who retrieved it.

"Midwest Medical Clinic," she said pursuing the contents.

"That was where I took my son," Mr. Zalbowski said finally taking a step into the room and coming toward the round oak table, his rumpled suit jacket hanging on his tired shoulders. The second button on his shirt was missing leaving behind only a tuff of white severed thread.

"Yes, I did a little research on them after Joseph told me about the clinic. Their building was paid for by Health American. An interesting fact, Health American is owed by Oxfam Medical Incorporated."

"And who are they?" Emily asked.

"Who indeed . . ." I raised a snarking eyebrow. "If you would Miss Haptonstall," I said indicating the large paper index on the book stand near the wall. ". . . that is if my systems are not too antiquated."

She gave me a slight sniff and proceeded to the large book index which I had compiled myself.

"But what does this have to do with my son?" Zalbowski said falling into one of the chairs at the table.

"I'm getting there Mr. Zalbowski," I answered. "Joseph . . . JOSEPH," finally throwing a pencil at him.

"What?" he croaked finally turning toward me. "You know nearly all your books were printed before 1950. The only ones printed after that are the ones you got from me . . ."

"Focus Joseph . . . we can discuss my library later."

"Still some of these must be worth," he mumbled. "This one . . . I haven't even seen a copy . . ."

"Joseph," I glared at him momentarily, until he put the book back on the shelf and crossed the room to the table, giving one last longing glance to the wall of books. I then turned back to Miss Haptonstall. "Oxfam Medical."

"Right," she grabbed a large chuck of pages, searching for the O's; struggling somewhat to turn the massive tome. "Oxfam . . . incorporated 1984 . . . owner of Body Plus, Cardiac Plus, Dental American, Family Physicians of Alberta, Health American, Living Good, Medical Rights, Medical Medright, Mediplux and Rx21 . . . a subsidiary of DG Industries . . ." she turned back to me.

"DG Industries," I said pointing back to the index book.

Struggling again, she turned back toward the front of the huge index. "DB . . . DD . . . DG . . . DG Industries . . . owned by LL Benjamin Carol . . . incorporated 1963 . . . owner of . . . there must be two pages here . . ." she looked back at me.

"Skip down to who owns them," I replied.

She ran her finger down the page and the next page and the next, and the next. ". . . a subsidiary of Leoda Pharmaceuticals . . ." Emily didn't wait she immediately began turning to the L's.

"Leoda . . . 1951 . . . subsidiary . . ." she turned the page.

"DG Leoda Incorporated," she began to turn the index once again without question.

"There's no need Miss Haptonstall," I said pausing her efforts. "DG Leoda Incorporated was founded in the late 1940's after the war. It was just one of dozens that appeared after the umbrella of IG Farben disintegrated after the war."

"IG Farben?" she questioned turning from the index.

"IG Farben was a massive cartel of businesses both in Germany and internationally. They gained massive industrial and economic control through both wars . . . World War I and World War II. Many believed IG Farben was a central point to the Nazis war machine and in 1946 during the Nuremberg Trials there was a call for an international military tribunal. But it collapsed and was left to individual trials of the industrial war criminals in each of the Allied zones of Germany.

The only thing was by the time prosecution of IG Farben's people began in 1947, the cold war had begun. The USSR who had been an ally was now an enemy . . . making Germany a strategic piece to be fought over . . . especially German business and scientific advancements . . . representatives in our own House quickly put pressure on prosecutors as to why we were continuing the trials of so called ordinary business men . . . as though they had done absolutely nothing during the war except carry a briefcase to work . . ." I paused. "Finally the trials ended . . . the few that were convicted got nothing more than a slap on the wrist . . . the highest punishment was eight years imprisonment for a conviction of mass murder . . ."

"My God," Emily injected.

I agreed but continued. "After that . . . pieces that had been IG

Farben were absorbed, shifted and destroyed. The companies that absorbed them all became bigger than IG at its zenith . . . and many are still with us today . . . not of course counting the numerous new companies that emerged, such as Leoda, or the already camouflaged American and foreign assets that went all the way through the war much of the time making profits on both sides of the Atlantic . . . at the expense or price of human lives," I broke off with a tempered snarl.

"Nazis," Joseph breathed out, sliding into a chair at the table next to Mr. Zalbowski. Who was already seated, listening and waiting for my words to somehow lead him to his son.

"Exactly, but perhaps more important to us are the men that helped establish DG Leoda after the war. They were all associates or employees of this man," I dropped a black and white photograph from the file I was holding, onto the table. "Dr. Delgado Ernst."

"Ernst," Emily returned, looking at the black and white photo of a rather distinguished looking man.

"Auschwitz," Mr. Zalbowski said.

"Delgado?" Joseph questioned.

"He was born in Mexico. His father was a German chemist, who was exploiting the untapped botanical riches of Central and South America. Delgado Ernst was born around 1911. Like Mengele his friend and colleague, he was trained under Professor Otmar Von Schedur at the Institute of Hereditary Biology. More importantly he became one of the over 350 doctors who experimented on the prisoners of the concentration camps, such as Auschwitz. The Nazi concept of racial hygiene . . . what was also called eugenics and later became modern genetics, was his primary devotion. Ernst was a focused man . . . and like Mengele was fascinated by twins . . . ."

I paused to take a breath. My eyes shifted to the black and white photo as a bile taste rose in my throat but I continued. ". . . but their main area was human survival, specifically the genetic instincts of survival and its hereditary factors."

"Wait . . . genetics? Wasn't DNA discovered by Watson and Crick around . . . 1950 or something?" Joseph questioned.

"Yes, but eugenics and heredity were around centuries before those two got in the game with the double helix . . ." I quickly returned. "Genetics goes back to the mid-1800's or before . . ."

"What about this . . . Ernst?" Emily questioned turning over the photo no longer wanting to see the face of the man they were all talking about.

"He would inject viral cocktails into prisoners then record the results . . . specifically the differences between twins . . ." I returned.

"But why is that important?" Emily questioned with a look of pained disgust.

"Because Ernst especially liked families and generations of families . . . picking them out of the lines as the trains pulled into the camps. His one regret was he couldn't carry out his theories over the long term . . . over generations . . . the full scope of his experiments were never exactly known . . . but what was known was enough . . ."

"And you think someone's continuing his work . . . Ernst's work . . ." Joseph said with a pronounced swallow.

"I know they are."

"How?" Emily questioned.

"Mr. Zalbowski . . . father to son, father to son . . . what Delgado Ernst always wanted. That's why they took Jeffrey and why they want you Mr. Zalbowski . . ."

"Nazis have my son?"

It was probably the worst thing I could have told him or anyone, but there was more and it was even worse than Nazis. "Nazi is a word . . . but the likes of Ernst were around long before the Nazis . . . using politics and people like pieces on a murderous sadistic chess board."

"Where is he?" Mr. Zalbowski asked sorrow dripping from his question.

"Where could they do something like this . . . hold a boy for a year experimenting on him . . ." Emily questioned doubt in her voice.

"A lot of places," Joseph replied. "There are highly secure private companies all over the country . . . most people don't even know they're there, but they're everywhere . . . in neighborhoods, in towns and cities. There was a really good article by this reporter in . . ."

"Joseph . . ." I stopped him from continuing. "Where . . ." I said stepping over to the large board Emily had been eyeing earlier and pulling down a large map of the country covered in tiny red dots. "My best guess here," I pointed to the map.

"Where?" Joseph questioned rising and coming closer.

"Here central Iowa . . . among genetically modified cornfields and pharmaceutical companies. Where the average citizen is on ten medication a day . . . the devil's playground."

"Iowa?" Emily scoffed.

"I knew there was always something hinky about that state," Joseph said beneath his breath.

"You've got to be kidding," Emily returned. "Iowa . . . there are rogue Nazi scientists experimenting on kidnapped children in Iowa . . . come on . . ."

"You read the companies . . . you saw the connections . . ." Joseph argued.

"This is worse than an urban myth or a conspiracy theory . . . and giving this man false hope is just . . ." Emily gestured to Zalbowski, who looked more horrified than stunned by the information. ". . . well it's despicable."

"Not false hope Miss Haptonstall. These people exist. They always have and unfortunately it may be they always will."

"You can't seriously think people would do this. It's been seventy years since the Nazis."

"You don't know what humans are capable of unless you've seen the death camps first hand," my ire was raised and I spoke out of turn, letting a little too much slip without forethought.

"Well you certainly haven't seen them . . . first hand Mr. Taylor and don't act as though you have," Emily argued back.

"Yeah Mel . . . you're only a few years older than me and I was born in the early seventies," Joseph added.

"I don't care about any of this," Mr. Zalbowski slapped his hand on the table, surprising all of us with the sudden force. "If there is a thread of chance my son is there . . . and alive I'm getting him."

"I agree Mr. Zalbowski," I returned. There was no theory too unbelievable if it meant there was even an infinitesimal hope of finding his son.

Joseph nodded.

Emily was silent, her eyes looking me up and down examining me with unspoken question.

We had all forgotten in our enthusiasm this was not about history or certainty. It was about a father and son. "I'm sorry Mr.

Zalbowski. We haven't forgotten about Jeffrey . . . but we can't just go get him. This will take time . . . I can only make an educated guess where he might be . . ."

"Can't we just call the police," Mr. Zalbowski offered.

"The police will have no jurisdiction and no judge will issue a search warrant on only open available corporate records . . . we don't know exactly where Jeffrey is . . ."

"Then what?" Mr. Zalbowski questioned in frustration.

"I'll figure that out . . . but first the most important thing is getting you somewhere safe Mr. Zalbowski . . . somewhere they can't find you," I offered him a sympathetic nod.

Mr. Zalbowski slumped back in his chair defeated and demoralized. His son was still out of reach.

"Miss Haptonstall?" I questioned noting her checking her watch and suddenly rising from the table.

"I'm afraid I have to go . . ." she said quietly stepping away from the table and Mr. Zalbowski.

"Go?" I questioned. "Is your hour up?" I snarked, then wished I hadn't.

"I have somewhere important I must be," she returned seeming not to have noticed my bad sarcasm.

"More important than a missing child and Nazis?" Joseph questioned with a half snarky stunned tone of his own.

"Miss Haptonstall," I started as she stepped away from the table.

"Part time remember, work from home," she looked at her watch once more. "I can't stay."

I followed her to the door.

"It was . . ." she hesitated. ". . . interesting. If you need my assistance call me . . . at home . . ." She was out the door and down the stairs before I could answer.

I followed her down but she had left before I even reached the bottom of my staircase. I could have been suspicious but who would leave before finding out where I was taking Mr. Zalbowski. No I probably wouldn't even hear from her again, our crazy talk of Nazis and kidnapped children was enough to scare anybody off, even a Haptonstall. I locked the back door and returned to the library.

"She's a weird one . . . pretty," Joseph raised an eyebrow. ". . . but weird . . ." I wasn't sure what it said about Joseph that he was taking this conspiracy of Nazis in Iowa so calmly, well as calmly as Joseph took anything.

"Your flyer," I returned with a shrug.

"Look," he turned his back to Mr. Zalbowski at the table and in a half whisper said. "I should probably call the Rose Tree and let them know I'm going to be out most of the day . . ."

"Go back to the Rose Tree Joseph. There's not much you can help with right now. I need to get Mr. Zalbowski someplace safe."

"But . . ." Joseph began disappointment in his voice. For the first time he was actually living something like he published. Dark conspiracies and half proven scenarios that shifted between reality and illusion that cut to truth and laid raw the wounds of unspoken history.

"Trust me Joseph, I'll call you if I need you. Or just show up around midnight . . ."

"Great . . ." he grunted with an almost pained expression on his face before walking back over to Mr. Zalbowski. Who was still seated at the table, his face drawn in focused fear. "Good luck . . . I believe you my friend. I believe you . . . good luck, Mel," he said and followed Miss Haptonstall's path down the staircase.

I guess nothing cleared a room quite as quickly as saying we were up against Nazis. They were right. To them it was history and not even their parents but their grandparents and great grandparents; to them it was seventy years . . . but to me it was more than half of my adult life.

We were suddenly all alone just me and Mr. Zalbowski, alone in a room of dark history, surrounded by the black and white statistics of evil. The same history and information I had spent over half my existence living and the other half piecing together. "Come on Mr. Zalbowski . . ." I said. ". . . let's see if we can get out of here."

CHAPTER NINE

After gathering everything I thought I might need into a backpack and my old leather wide mouth bag, we cautiously once again headed for my car.

"You need to stop having those parties at night," the elderly black man yelled from his porch on the other side of my gravel drive.

"It wasn't a party, Mr. Delmar," I returned without looking to see him glaring from the front porch of his house. Mr. Delmar was nigh on ancient. He had a receding diamond of white hair that claimed the top of his head like a small island separated from the mainland of his hair. His life now consisted of vocal orders shouted from his perched observation of any and all who had the misfortune to step within the visual comfort of his house's porch. Yet even for his age he was spry. Spry enough to mow his yard three or four times a week and use the remaining time keeping a leering eye on me.

"Too much damn noise . . . and when are you going to mow that weed patch you call a yard back there . . ." he bellowed, his finger jutting in accusing fashion toward the back of my property.

"Soon Mr. Delmar," I replied, intending to let the grass grow as long as I could, and got in my car after filling the tank with a jug of water. I could feel Mr. Delmar's narrowed eyes disapproving of whatever he thought I was doing. I pulled forward in my gravel drive. Mr. Zalbowski was sitting quietly in the back seat, silent and almost childlike. His hands folded his head down in his depression and worry. That would throw Mr. Delmar into convulsions I could see him shaking his head vigorously on the porch and cursing, as I looked up and down the street. I hadn't spotted the blue Volkswagen or anyone else on my first trip to the car with my bags but I wasn't taking any chances. "Lay down in the seat Mr. Zalbowski at least till we're outside the cities. Hopefully if they see us they may think I left you in my house . . ." which I guess didn't bode well for my house.

Zalbowski did as I said, causing Mr. Delmar to lean over his porch railing to get a better view. He teetered slightly but kept from falling all the way over onto the ground. I pulled out into the busy afternoon traffic. The August sun was burning through the windshield, but luckily the humidity had subsided some over night making it balmy but not boiling.

There might not have been a blue Volkswagen, but I didn't see the gray SUV pull out two streets away on the opposite side of the road and slink slowly behind us into the traffic.

ɔͼɔ

"Mrs. Rayburn," Emily called closing the front door to her compact little single level colonial house. The outside of the house was painted white with robin egg blue trim surrounded by a white picket fence and a well manicured lawn. The most unconventional thing about the little grandmotherly looking house not that it was very unconventional, was a two year old red Japanese maple on the left side of the front lawn. It looked like a grandmother's house because it was or at least it had been. Emily's parents had died in a traffic accident when she was only fifteen that was when she and her sister had come to live with their grandmother.

Elizabeth, Emily's sister, or E as Emily called her was ten years her junior. Elizabeth had medical problems, problems that weren't exactly run of the mill. She had been diagnosed as epileptic as a child, even though she wasn't a classic epileptic. It would be the first in a long list of diagnosed syndromes and diseases that Elizabeth would have placed upon her. She was intelligent but seemed to remain almost childlike. She had un-diagnosised bouts of seizures not related to the epilepsy, at least that was what the doctors had said, and severe often times violent mood swings. Between Emily and her grandmother they had kept Elizabeth protected and happy with minimal need for invasive medical, social or government interference. Even when their grandmother's health had begun failing, she had held on long enough for Emily to inherit the little well ordered house and take over as legal guardian of her younger sister Elizabeth.

"Mrs. Rayburn?" Emily called once again.

"Yes child, in the kitchen," came the reply.

Mrs. Rayburn was a neighbor and dear friend of their grandmother, who often stayed with Elizabeth when Emily needed to go out for groceries or work. Their parent's life insurance had built a hefty nest egg of financial stability but even Emily knew it wouldn't last forever; and rather than cut into their savings Emily kept enough money coming in to pay most of the expenses. Most of her work consisted of employment over the internet, so she could be home with Elizabeth, such as Mr. Taylor's part time employ. But Emily had other reasons for wanting to obtain the job with Mr. Taylor, something her grandmother had told Emily before her death. Something Emily still wasn't sure about, how or what it all meant.

"Hello Mrs. Rayburn," Emily said coming into the generously windowed kitchen.

"Hello dear, just finishing a batch of cookies for Elizabeth," Mrs. Rayburn said. The elderly woman was thin but still held a wiriness about her that had no doubt been extensive in her youth. Her white hair was bundled up in a roll at the back of her head with a stray occasional lock roaming free and unruly. She was still quite a tall woman even for her age.

"How has she been?" Emily questioned.

"Very calm today, it is a good day."

"I'm sorry I'm late. I didn't expect it to take so long," Emily replied.

"I understand dear," Mrs. Rayburn answered arranging the warm cookies on a plate then straightening her cream cardigan. It was a hot August day but he still always seemed to be wearing one. "I keep telling you anytime. I'm willing to sit with Elizabeth. I can handle her surprises . . . ."

"I know . . ." Emily said. ". . . and thank you Mrs. Rayburn."

"You need to get out more dear," Mrs. Rayburn called after Emily as she went to find Elizabeth.

"E," Emily said with a soft tone slowly opening the door and entering her sister's room to find Elizabeth sitting by the window dazing out into the dappling sunlight. Her fingers playing at the window sill and the tiny ceramic horse Elizabeth had possessed since childhood.

"Emily," her sister smiled back. Her coloring was quite similar to Emily's, dark auburn hair perhaps a shade or too lighter, warm pink cheeks that matched her pink lips and pale blue eyes, eyes not quite as deep and steely gray blue as Emily's. Elizabeth was petite and thin, but her size could fool you. She was no weakling and when the episodes of violence struck, she had on more than one occasion injured Emily quite severely.

"Mrs. Rayburn says you've been enjoying yourself," Emily spoke with a soft tone, coming closer to her sister.

"I have . . . I swung in the yard all morning . . . but now the shadows have come," she looked out toward the swing with a deep frown.

Emily looked out at the swing which was cast in the bright rays of sun. The shadows Elizabeth spoke of were not from lack of sunlight.

"I don't like it when the shadows come."

"I know you don't E," Emily returned. "But they always leave. The shadows always leave," she offered her sister a small smile.

"I know . . . Grandma says the shadows are angry."

Emily grimaced. "We talked about this E. You know Grandma isn't here . . ."

Elizabeth looked down at the window sill, her pink lips pouting. She didn't like it when Emily scolded her about speaking to their grandmother as though she was still alive. "But . . ." Elizabeth began to protest.

Emily gave her sister a soft hug. "Mrs. Rayburn has made cookies. Why don't you go see if they're ready."

Elizabeth smiled, hugged her sister. "You like your new job . . ."

Emily gave her sister a half smile in return. She wasn't sure what to think of Mr. Taylor and her new job. His situation was . . . odd to say the least. Emily wasn't sure whether she was even doing the right thing. What they had discussed . . . had been . . . well crazy.

Elizabeth looked at her sister. "Grandma approves . . ." she said and merrily headed for the kitchen following the trail of sweet baking aromas.

Emily could only hope their grandmother would approve. It was a good day, Emily thought. She had been hugged and received a smile and even a coherent conversation. If only every day could go as well, Emily pondered.

She glanced out the window to the single tree swing, beneath the large walnut tree, now cloaked in long shadows, from a stray cloud crossing the sky. She caught the sad expression of her own features in the glass and stepped away. She could wish for things to change, but she knew they never would.

Mrs. Rayburn was helping Elizabeth to cookies as Emily passed into her own bedroom. It had been a strange morning, not exactly what she had expected. She sat down on her bed and reached over, opening a small wooden box on her night stand. She looked at the old series of letters bound with a slightly frayed and faded ribbon. Emily didn't bother picking them out of the box she just slowly closed the lid and set it back on the night stand.

"I still don't understand, Grandma," Emily said. "What does Mr. Taylor have to do with anything?"

ᕮᕲ

Joseph finally looked presentable. He had showered, shaved and put on a new clean pair of pants. He had only slept a few hours last night and the late afternoon was starting to wear on him. He'd made the schedules out for his lawn service, returned two phone calls he'd missed that morning, approved three book covers before their run and was now sitting at his desk in the publishing building staring mindlessly at the large fish tank on the other side of his office. The blue and yellow cichlids darted about in the shimmering lighted tank between the thick flat rocks, the gurgling water permeating his unraveling thoughts.

Had they actually discussed what they had discussed this morning... Nazis, death camps, kidnapped children, experiments. A sudden shudder ran though him. Everyday he dealt with conspiracies and lies. Two of the current titles that they were in the works of publishing dealt with Nazis and the war.

He knew it was probably true but believing that they were tangibly near his everyday life was more than unsettling. It was frightening. He thought of Mr. Zalbowski and Jeffrey and couldn't help but wonder. How many of his own relatives had died in the concentration camps. He knew his parents and grandparents, his immediate family had been in the United States for generations, but what about their brothers and sisters, nieces and nephews, cousins and uncles.

There was a knock at his door. He flinched in startled shock.

"I'm sorry . . . Mr. Morgenstein," Tanya, his assistant, had entered and was standing before him. Her head titled slightly as she looked at him with kind blue eyes, her curving red hair falling to the side of her head in soft waves.

"Tanya," he said breaking his maudlin musing.

"Mr. Taxon has been trying to reach you," she handed him a note with Taxon's telephone number and the times which he had previously called. "He called this morning something about the order for new shelving . . . I told him you'd call . . ."

"Yes, of course . . . thank you Tanya," Joseph replied, picking up his phone, only to return it to its cradle a second later. He wasn't ready yet to deal with business.

"Are you alright sir," Tanya began, then suddenly feeling perhaps her question was out of place . . . even though they were basically about the same age, but he was still her boss. "It's just you're usually more . . . energetic," she shrugged.

"I suppose I'm just a little tired," Joseph replied.

"Was it Mr. Taylor?" she questioned.

"Sort of . . ." Joseph returned.

"Is he alright? He looked quite . . ."

"I guess he looked a bit shocking . . . how is everyone?" Joseph asked recalling Mel's bloody, beaten appearance.

"Mrs. Robinson can't stop talking about it . . . which is somewhat a blessing since she's finally stopped talking about her flooring."

Joseph chuckled. Two weeks ago Mrs. Robinson had replaced all the carpet in her home. There had not been a quiet moment since, every minute detail had been relived in vivid and often painful color. The installer had not met her rigid expectations.

"What happened? I mean to Mr. Taylor?" Tanya questioned.

"Mrs. Robinson said he came back again . . . and there were other people with him . . . a man . . . and a young woman?" she paused. It wasn't her business. She shouldn't be asking . . . but he seemed almost upset about something since Mr. Taylor's abrupt visits.

Joseph hesitated. How exactly could he explain the last few hours. A lot of it was still unbelievable to him.

"It's not important . . ." she smiled. ". . . so long as everyone's ok," Tanya returned seeing Joseph was having trouble summing up whatever had happened. "Don't forget Mr. Taxon . . ." she said and turned to leave.

"I should call him shouldn't I . . ." Joseph said with a sigh looking at the phone.

Tanya turned back toward Joseph's desk. "If you like I can call him . . . you already decided what we needed to order . . ." she offered, her kind eyes and bright porcelain features looking at him.

He could. Joseph knew he could let her. He trusted her implicitly. In many ways Tanya Kelley knew the Rose Tree's three businesses as well if not better that he did. She was far more than what the lowly moniker of her title assistant described her.

"No . . . I've put him off three times . . . I should really be the one to talk to him . . ." Joseph finally returned, picking up the phone once again.

Tanya gave him another soft smile and turned to leave.

Joseph paused a minute, the phone still in his hand taking a needed moment of beauty in Tanya's graceful departure.

CHAPTER TEN

I didn't doubt Brandon and Tabitha Forrester would want to help Mr. Zalbowski, but I was taking a pretty big chance involving them in this. There had already been two attempts on Mr. Zalbowski's life, or at least two attempts to kidnap him. I wasn't including the bruiser that had nearly diced me in two. I didn't want to involve the Forrester's, after what they'd gone through with their own boys. I didn't want to put them in danger, but I had no other place or people I trusted as much as the Forrester's.

Luckily the setting sun hadn't been in my eyes the entire trip to the Forrester's farm. Slowly the giant bright orb was disappearing into the cornfields as twilight started to claim the edges of the horizon. Hollow Tree Farm was up ahead. I glanced in the rear view mirror at Mr. Zalbowski. He hadn't said a word since we'd left the cities. He didn't have to his expression said it all. The poor guy had the dour, glum cloud of a thousand miseries across his face. I knew it well. It was as though someone had dropped a grenade in the center of your universe. Sure the initial blast and shrapnel was tremendous, deafening, injuring but that wasn't what hurt the most. It was the cracks. Long jagged hair line fractures so thin at first they were barely noticeable over the pumping adrenaline and fear. But slowly they got bigger, wider, chasms that began to consume the stability beneath your feet until everything that you once believed was swallowed into unfathomable darkness beneath you and you found yourself falling in nothingness. The gentle roll of the car was his metronome now and when it stopped I feared he would realize the world he knew had slipped away. At least, I thought, if Jeffrey was alive he had him to center on, and maybe something on which to rebuild a new universe.

✩

Brandon met us before I had even shut off the engine. His large rounded shoulders silhouetted in the growing darkness spoke of a life of hard hand labor lived in sun warmed farm fields. Brandon was a large man six foot two in stocking feet, with boots he towered over most. He had burnished sandy hair and a face that belonged in the old west. Honest and strong, it showed the health and soulful fulfillment of a hard day's work.

"Back already," he called. He was setting up his large telescope in one of the few areas near the farm house not teeming with vigorous growing plants overwhelmed by slowly ripening produce.

"Yeah," I replied stepping out of the car, avoiding the cat that had come to investigate my arrival. I glanced at Mr. Zalbowski. Who had only just realized the car had stopped. I twisted my lips as Brandon approached wondering what to say. I took his well calloused strong hand in greeting. "I need to ask a favor."

"It's yours whatever, you know that . . . we owe you two beautiful sons," he answered giving his rolled up sleeves another push.

"Yeah, ummm . . ." I stepped away from the car grasping Brandon's shoulder and leading him out of earshot of the car. "About that," I looked back at Mr. Zalbowski. ". . . that's Mr. Zalbowski . . . someone's taken his son and now they're after him. I need someplace to stash him while I try and locate the boy."

Brandon looked to the back seat of my car. It was lit in bright contrasts of yellow illumination and shadowed darkness from the light above one of the out buildings and the consuming evening. The stocky, short, little man looked older than his years. His wire rimmed glasses sliding down his nose, his posture slumped and listless.

"You don't have to ask twice . . ." Brandon said. "He's welcome here."

"Thanks Brandon . . . you need to be aware though . . . there are some pretty nasty people after him . . . I mean the worst of the worst. I could be putting your family in danger," I hesitated to accept his generous offer.

"Brandon," Tabitha called from the porch with a squeak of the screen door. "Is that Mel?" she said switching on the porch light to illuminate the brown beast.

"You need to talk to your wife," I said waving to Tabitha with a smile.

"You just said you didn't have any other place to go . . ." Brandon looked at me with a disapproving expression.

I shook my head. "You say no . . . I'll figure something out." I had no idea what that was going to be, but I wasn't going to force the

Forrester's into endangering themselves just to help me. Even though I realized that was exactly what I was asking. Maybe I should just turn around now and leave before . . .

"I don't have to ask Tabitha, I know what she'll say," Brandon replied.

"Ask her anyway," I returned feeling guilty about needing their help and even guiltier that I might be hanging Mr. Zalbowski out to dry. I rubbed my stiff neck and even stiffer back and returned to the brown beast. Brandon walked to the porch and started conversing with Tabitha. I was still leaning on the brown beast when Tabitha came off the porch a few minutes later.

She walked to the other side of the car without a word to me and opened the door to Mr. Zalbowski.

"Would you please come inside Mr. Zalbowski, I'm sure you could use a nice meal and some rest." She was right. As Mr. Zalbowski slowly got out of my car I noted his boyish soft jowls held a days worth of dark gray beard, far grayer and whiter than the dark curls of his receding widow's peek. There was an almost reticent motion to his limbs as he forced them to move forward even though he didn't want to go any farther. I couldn't imagine. His son had been missing for almost a year. His only son, his wife had died and now . . . his son was the man's only family.

Tabitha Forrester led Mr. Zalbowski toward the house. Her arm softly wrapped about his shorter shoulders in motherly comfort. Brandon and Tabitha were good folks if only the world was filled with more of them.

"Do you need any help?" Brandon questioned once they were inside the white farm house.

"No but thanks . . . just keep your eye out . . . hell keep both eyes out . . ." I said climbing back in my car.

"Do I want to ask what you're going to do?" he looked at me through the open window.

"Best not . . ." I answered.

"What about where you're going . . . ?"

I didn't answer.

"How do you get roped into these things?" Brandon scoffed.

"I just try to help . . ." I returned. ". . . and the less you know the better."

"And we're glad you do . . ." Brandon offered. "Good luck . . ."

"I just hope I can find his son," I replied but maybe what I really hoped was that Jeffrey was alive.

Brandon patted the top of the brown beast twice and I pulled off into the night, leaving the warm golden light of the white farm house and the Forrester's of Hollow Tree Farm behind me. I had about a hundred miles to cross before I reached Leoda Pharmaceuticals. It was one of the most isolated buildings in the giant Leoda Company's holdings. It was close. It was secure. It was basically secret and I couldn't think of a better place to hide a kid for almost a year without anybody finding him. Yet have it still be close enough to go after Mr. Zalbowski with a coordinated attack; at least that's what I was going for . . . it was my best clue, hell it was my only clue. Worse I didn't have a damn plan. Not that I was new to that sort of situation either, but what I was going to do once I got there . . . well that was as much of a guess to me as anyone.

However not having a plan had never stopped me before actually most of my plans seemed to be *not* to have a plan. So I was right on course with the way the rest of my life had gone, because it had gone so well so far . . . if you could say such a thing about time travel. I knew the place would have security, no doubt some of the tightest in the world. Here I was blindly driving into urban myth and conspiracy theory territory . . . . I was ready to start kicking some sand around in the devil's playground. I was searching for Nazis in the Iowa cornfields.

CHAPTER ELEVEN

It was the deep dark part of the night now, no longer the soft twilight of a couple of hours ago. For an hour I had been accompanied by no other sounds except the crunch of my tires on the gravel farm roads and the cooled wind of the late summer breezes through my open car window. The thing about the country and cornfields is it's easy to get turned around and lost. Signs are few and far between and landmarks, well if you eliminate the corn there isn't much else. If they had planned to hide the place they'd done a good job. No one would continue this far out expecting to find . . . I stopped the car. There was a glow in the distance, like stadium lights on a baseball field. I crept quietly forward, the crunch of gravel suddenly turning to smooth cement beneath my wheels. A long anonymous drive led gullet like down into a swath of tall corn. It had to be now didn't it when the corn was at its height. When I couldn't see a damn thing for miles except the eerie flapping identical leaves of corn stocks. It was a mirage like shifting green tasseled sand, row upon row until directions blurred into mazes of confusion.

I paused a long moment preparing myself. I licked my lips and proceeded down the drive. Abruptly the cornfields ended, replaced by flat perfectly manicured grass topped overhead by tall poles of flood lights. The complex beyond was massive. Large connecting rectangles of steel gray and cement white emerged from the perfectly manicured or rather controlled landscape. Not a blade of grass dared to be out of line. I could see every sharp vertical and horizontal line of the building, every window and walkway, every blade of grass. The flood lights were creating the artificial atmosphere of day. I hadn't expected the number of people, well I assumed people since the number of cars parked in front of the building were too numerous to count even at this hour. I hadn't realized how long I had sat there idling, staring at the manifest mirage in the middle of the cornfields, until a security guard was standing in front of my car. A rather intimidating assault weapon strapped to his armored chest and all black uniform. Crap.

"Mr. Taylor."

I swallowed had he just said my name.

"Mr. Taylor, please pull forward we've been expecting you."

Double crap.

I pulled slightly forward. Yeah I did. I mean what else was I going to do. I'd driven this far. There was no point in turning around now. Ok maybe there were a lot of points, guards, guns, lights, building, Nazis. But who was I to ever bend to convention.

"If you'd pull to the front of the building sir, Dr. Cox will meet with you there," a second guard spoke to me as I pulled to a stop before the barred square black metal gate.

"Dr. Cox?" I questioned. I couldn't help but notice the rather large side arm the guard was carrying along with the assault rifle. Yeah, pharmaceuticals that's what they did here. Apparently their quickest method of injection was with a bullet. Guaranteed to provide the ultimate cure for all the problems of life . . . death.

"Yes sir," the young man said with authoritative efficiency. I got the feeling he was ex-military with the cropped hair and muscular toned bare forearms. I'd seen a lot of guys like him. Old enough to be out of the military after going in as essentially a kid only to come out still needing the structure of someone else to keep giving him orders to follow. Eventually ending up working security for some off the books project where deniability was paramount and where unbeknownst to them, guys like him were expendable. He waved a commanding hand for me to proceed.

I felt as though I'd just fallen down the rabbit hole. I passed through the gated fence, a fence that appeared to cage the entire massive complex. I had the feeling it wasn't deer they were trying to keep out. Then over what I could only describe as a moat then through another gate. I don't know if the brown beast was scared as much as I was but as we crossed the moat, she gave a small yet audible pop. I didn't blame her. There was no way we were getting back out of here easily if they tried to stop us. I stopped at the front of the massive building. More security greeted me and by greet I mean glared while they held quite impressive weapons; all shiny and black under the large lights. I didn't know whether to be impressed that they felt I was that dangerous or be scared that there were so many, ready and armed. I mentioned they were all armed right, really armed and not with nice little side arms like the one I'd stuck in my jacket before driving down the last of the gravel road. I didn't like guns . . . hell who does . . . but I really didn't like their guns. These were scary looking semi-automatics with clip magazines wrapped about their bulky Kevlar encased chests. I was in a t-shirt. I thought I'd go with impressed. Yeah, they were scared of me I told myself trying not to shake as I got out of the car.

"Mr. Taylor," a rather thin man with a wispy comb of hay colored hair greeted me. His suit was gray but obviously expensive. It probably cost more than I'd spent in a year. "Dr. Lewis T. Cox . . ." he paused as if expecting recognition before offering his well manicured hand in greeting.

I scratched my ear and kept my hands to myself. I make it a policy to never shake the hand of someone who might be a Nazi. There's not a soap in the world that can clean that off.

"Of course," he said seeming slightly snubbed by my lack of common etiquette. "I believe you have come a short distance . . . in a very long moment of time . . ." he tilted his head and gave me a generous smile which unnerved me.

I took a little closer notice maybe this guy wasn't just a greeting wagon after all.

"I would offer you a truce, but my associates fear the effort would be wasted on someone lacking the proper vision . . ."

"Vision . . ." I returned. That was an insult, I should feel insulted.

"Besides I am told you are thoroughly versed in our various endeavors first hand . . . albeit . . . your awareness is behind the times."

Ok that's the second not so veiled reference to time. The hairs on the back of my neck were rising higher. I didn't like vague innuendos when I had no idea what or who I was dealing with or what the innuendos were in reference to . . . why couldn't bad guys speak plainly.

"I'd like to meet your associates," I returned. "Any of them happen to be around . . ."

"Around . . . about . . . I'm sure you'll meet them some*time*," he said in a calm tone. His dark eyes never shifting from me. "Until then I have been authorized to provide you with information. You may ask anything you wish. You may not however receive every answer," he finished with a gleeful smile.

Swell I thought, my own personal Nazi genie. My lip gave a twisted snarl. "Ok . . . do you have the Zalbowski boy?"

Cox pondered a moment then answered. "Yes," he replied calmly.

"Is he here?"

"No."

"Where is he?"

Cox smiled. His dark eyes seemed to sparkle as if the question amused him and this was all just a game. A fixed game he knew he was winning. "He is not . . . in the present."

Odd way to put it. "Is he alive?"

"Yes."

"I don't suppose you'll just hand him over."

"No."

"What will I need to get him back?"

"Time, Mr. Taylor, time."

I glared. Ok the guy was starting to piss me off. "Who took him?"

"Men, simply men."

"Stooges. No I mean who gave the orders for the boy to be taken? You?" I grunted.

"My associates," he answered still maintaining a false politeness.

"Do your associates have names?" I was starting to sweat. It was cool but under the blazing flood lights the cool night breezes felt like memories of a distance place, where other black clad men had once surrounded me with guns.

"Oh of course they do, Mr. Taylor."

I gnawed at the inside of my mouth. "I don't suppose you'd tell me any of their names."

"You know their names . . ." Cox smiled again.

The statue warrior guardians were making me nervous. How long could I ask questions, more importantly how long till I became just another spot cleaned off the sidewalk. I looked down at the almost white cement. Cox wasn't telling me anything. What he was telling me was making me twitch.

"What's the point to my asking questions if I'm not getting any answers."

"Ask the right questions Mr. Taylor," Cox returned.

"Why take the boy?"

"You already know that answer, Mr. Taylor. It led you here."

"Ernst, Auschwitz," I answered.

Cox was silent, but he didn't flinch or correct me. Were these the same people who I'd fought more than sixty years ago. The same people I'd gone against my own government to try and stop. I thought I'd stopped them in 1948. I should have known better.

"Will you kill the boy? The father?"

"Time is your answer Mr. Taylor. I cannot stress that enough. The boy is part of that now. The father is currently all but expendable . . . unless circumstances change. He was a means to an end, as the boy is. Their main purpose . . . for now is done. They had perhaps only one major purpose left."

"Which was?" I frowned.

"Bringing you here," he returned, his eyes staring directly at me.

I thought about it. If the boy and Mr. Zalbowski weren't important then they were just pawns, pieces to be moved around getting the other pieces on the board into place. Pieces like me.

"Has it dawned on you Mr. Taylor?"

I frowned.

"I was told to expect more . . ." Cox sniffed. "You seem far less significant than I was led to believe . . ."

"I ask the questions remember," I growled realizing I had been used. The whole Leoda Pharmaceuticals, the clinic, the missing boy everything bread crumbs to get my slow witted self to follow. I was a pawn and Cox and whoever his boss was . . . was moving me around their game board.

"It took you far longer than we expected . . . to become aware of the boy . . ."

"Aware? Why did you go after Mr. Zalbowski?" I growled. "Why the boy?" I grabbed Cox by the front of his expensive suit and tie. The statues came alive. About three cold barrels of steel touched my face. Two others pointed into my torso.

"If only you could see the bigger picture . . . if only you knew your place in events . . ."

"What are you talking about?" I growled, the barrels of the guns pressing tighter.

"Time is your guide Mr. Taylor," Cox returned. He seemed unflustered, amused even, though his face was turning a bit pink.

"You have an opportunity to get what you want. As we have one to get what we desire . . . convergences are required . . . now as in the past. You have made enemies Mr. Taylor, some who do not forget the passage of years. The father and son will die when the time is right . . ." he smiled. ". . . so will the twins."

"Twins?" my eyes flashed with anger. There was only one thing he could mean. I dropped Cox. His feet slipped back to the ground. I ran back to my car not once worrying about the statues and their weapons. I was worried about my friends.

"Let him go," Cox commanded. Straightening his suit and readjusting his tie as my brown beast sped past the two open entrances and disappeared into the night and the swallowing cornfield maze. "He's going exactly where he's supposed to . . . finally."

CHAPTER TWELVE

I got lost twice on the damn country back roads among the cornfields, trying to get back to the river and out of Iowa. By the time I crossed the bridge I had sworn through I think two entire counties, using words that would have made a drill sergeant blush.

Mr. Zalbowski and his son would die and so would the twins. I raced off the interstate. Luckily it was late in the evening and there was little traffic. Even luckier no state police to stop me. I thought if something happened to the Forrester's, to Brandon and Tabitha, to the twins . . . it would be my fault. There was no way of getting around it, my fault. I couldn't live with that, not again. I knew better. I should never have involved them. I should have realized I was being played. That Mr. Zalbowski was just a lure. A lure to get me involved . . . but why? It had taken me a year to become aware of Jeffrey Zalbowski that was what Cox said. Everything was trying to lead me somewhere but why. I missed a curve and nearly ended up in a drainage ditch. Gravel pinged against the metal undercarriage of my car and I heard clinking glass as rocks struck the back window.

It had been hours, would I be too late. Had everything already happened. What would I do if I walked in to find them all . . . I took out an old mail post as I pulled into Hollow Tree Farm. I felt the impact of the concrete filled metal post, but I didn't care what it did to the car. I didn't care if I killed the damn car. I would run the rest of the way if I had too. I shrieked to a halt.

The front door was open, warm yellow light was flooding out the screen door. Dozens of attracted moths and insects hovered near the light. I ran onto the porch, causing a cat hidden in the darkness to leap away with a hissing growl. I slipped on something sticky and wet. I grabbed the porch rail to keep myself from falling. I reached down to touch the dark substance and cast my hand into the yellow light. It was blood.

"Brandon! Tabitha!" I yelled yanking the screen door open and rushing inside. The living room was a disaster. Overturned tables and broken lamps lay among ripped up magazines and books. Children's drawing and crayons lay scattered. Their bright colored wax pulverized into the wooden floor. Worst of all there were drops of blood visible on many of the surfaces. I chocked back a feeling of sickness when I saw one of the twin's stuffed animals on the floor smeared with blood. I walked into the kitchen, the broken askew clock on the wall read 12:34. Damn it. "Brandon!" I called again, "Tabitha!" this time slower reluctantly realizing that there would probably be no response. There was a tray of fresh baked scones on the stove. The oven was still on but the scones were cold. More a large butcher knife lay on the floor the tip red with blood. Tabitha had fought back. Moving farther toward the back door I found Brandon's shotgun, I picked it up. There was still an unfired shell in the barrel. The dispersal pattern of the first shot fired had peppered the wall near the back door, where a window had been blown out. They had come in this way.

I sat down at the kitchen table. They were all gone. The chirping symphony of cicada echoed in loud drowning calls through the open back doorway. It was the only sound in miles. The house for all its shocking brightness seemed very empty and lifeless.

Suddenly I heard a cracking pounding from the basement. The shotgun was still in my hand as I ran down the stairs, my feet thundering against the boards. I brought the shotgun up with aiming purpose as I hit the bottom of the steps.

"Brandon!" I exclaimed finding him tied to a broken chair that had obviously been thrown down the basement stairs with him tied to it.

He groaned loudly and thrashed once more against the electric wires holding him. They appeared to have been pulled from the broken lamps upstairs. I dropped to my knees and laid the shotgun aside. Quickly I pulled off his gag. His face was a swollen mound. There was a severe cut to his left eyebrow and another to his temple and jaw.

"Brandon, what happened?"

"They took them. They took Tabitha, the boys . . . and your friend," he sputtered and coughed with a dry wheeze and a grimace of pain.

"Who?"

Brandon continued struggling against the wires as I pulled out my pocket knife to cut him loose.

"I don't know. There were six of them . . ." he coughed spitting blood this time onto the floor. Cutting him free I helped him to his feet. He wobbled slightly, grabbing at his side. More than one of his ribs had probably been cracked or broken from the fall down the stairs if the condition of the chair was any indication. "Upstairs," he chocked sputtering back his cough and grabbing his ribs.

"Come on man," I said helping him to his feet and up the steep stairs, finally depositing him in a chair at the kitchen table with a moan. In the bright lights Brandon looked even worse. Blood canvassed his shirt and pants. His wrists were bruised with deep lines that gouged his lacerated flesh where they had cut as he fought against the restraints.

"The main one, the leader . . ." he hacked. ". . . told me something . . . he said you would know what it meant . . . that if I wanted to save my family I had to remember . . ."

"What?" I returned, steadying him with my arm.

"He said . . . if you want to save a family, to save twin brothers . . . the answer to history is time . . ." Brandon coughed harder more blood crested his lips. He was in pain. ". . . then he wrote that . . ." Brandon pointed his shaking finger at the large kitchen window, his head dropping in agony as he did so. The blackness of the night outside obscured the dark lettering. I stepped closer. I couldn't read it. Grabbing the silver cookie sheet, I dumped the scones onto the counter. I raised the window and shoved the sheet inside against the screen and brought the window back down.

I read the dark words written in blood. Apple. Sunset.

"Do you know what they mean?" Brandon questioned with a wince. "Do you know where my family is?" he coughed.

I didn't answer. I knew what it meant. Apple. It wasn't a thing or a person. It was a place. It was a place I hadn't been in a very long time; a very, very long time.

"I know where they are," I finally replied, the color draining from my face. I almost wished I didn't.

"Where? . . . . Mel . . . ?"

For a moment I couldn't hear Brandon's groans. I was lost in a memory from years before, in a place from years before. A time that had set me on a path. A path that was now my history.

"Mel?" Brandon questioned with a growling moan before doubling over onto the floor.

I turned back to him. "I need to get you to a hospital."

"No, not until I find my family," Brandon moaned with increasing pain.

"Don't be a fool, your ribs are probably broken . . . you could have internal bleeding . . ."

"Not until . . ." he started.

"I'll find your family. It was my fault this happened." I took hold of Brandon trying to lift him off the floor. He cried out in agony. His arm was apparently also broken.

"No," he grunted, falling into the chair again. "I'm not going anywhere . . ." he spit up more blood onto the shiny surface of the kitchen table. ". . . just call 911," he groaned.

I dialed and handed Brandon the phone. There was no need for the police to know I was in the house. I went back over to the window. I picked up a cutting board and proceeded to break out the glass, destroying the words that had been written on it.

"Why did you do that?" Brandon asked, holding the mouth piece away from his face and coughing.

"I don't want any police getting in the way . . . you ok?" I questioned indicating the phone.

"I'll survive," he grunted spitting up a little more blood as he said it. "Get out of here . . . go save my family."

I hesitated as he spoke back into the phone to the 911 operator.

"Go," he said once more, his eyes pleading with me to save his family, no matter what the cost was to himself. I complied running out of the house and into my car.

ℤℤ

I checked my speed coming into the cities and slowed down to a reasonably accelerated race. The biggest thing concerning me besides what condition Tabitha, the twins and Mr. Zalbowski were in was who the hell could be behind all of this. I was ninety-five years old how could anyone I knew still be alive.

You are, I thought, yeah but I didn't count. I was an anomaly. I had seen to that. What had happened to me could never happen again, the device had been destroyed. Lives had been lost but I had stopped it. How I had even survived was a question.

I had waited for the ambulance to arrive for Brandon, sitting in the parked car hiding in a dark strip at the end of the road to Hollow Tree Farm. I told myself I had to wait, had to make sure Brandon would be alright, that the paramedics would get there soon enough to save him. I knew how slow county emergency response could be. More though I had needed time. Time mostly to process the shock that someone knew who I was. It wasn't just that they knew my name or were acquainted with me or even knew I was still alive.

Choosing Apple said they knew everything about me, even things my best friends had never known. No one knew about Apple, no one. Other than the people who were there, no one except, one other person and he was dead. He had died in my own arms. I shuddered at that pain. But this was laying raw something older, something I hadn't dealt with in decades. What had happened in Apple eighty-one years ago . . . the death of my own brother.

ⓒⓧⓢ

I pulled into my gravel driveway, the first rays of the morning sun cutting through the back window of my old car. Tiny stars from the broken glass scattered light burning with intensity against the divots and cracks the gravel impact had etched into my back window. The warm glow, the angle, the time of year, it all mirrored the morning I had found Sanford, my brother. It was palpable. I swear I smelled the hay mixed with the earthy animal smells of the old barn. I shook my head. Come on man you have the living to deal with, the living to save. But I could feel it, every step, every heartbeat.

I had less than twenty-four hours until sunset. Apple had still been a town maybe sixty years ago although calling it a town even then was a bit generous. Mostly it had consisted of a few farm houses that had called it home amongst apple orchards. But even sixty years ago the town had all but disappeared. It was simply unincorporated fields out in the middle of an Illinois county.

I wasn't sure what to expect but whoever it was; it was someone who knew my past and that frightened me more than anything.

They would never have chosen Apple unless they knew who I was and they knew me intimately.

I pushed the car door open, stepping out with my leather wide mouth bag in hand. Mr. Delmar was already roosting on his porch, his eyes intense and watching, examining and judging my every move. No doubt he disapproved of my early arrival and I thought coming around to the front of my car, noting the crumbled front headlight that was torn away from the car frame, he would disapprove of this as well. The mail post had done some pretty significant damage. The headlight was broken. The metal slightly smashed and scored. The massive chrome bumper of the thick old car was even dented. I had hit it hard. I patted the brown old beast kindly then walked toward the front of my building. I noted the paint of the g in genealogist was completely gone. I was now officially an eneaologist. Who knows maybe it would pay more, something so exotic. I fished through my keys and opened the door.

"Mr. Taylor . . ."

I groaned as I heard my name called. I didn't have to look to see who it was calling to me at this early an hour. I had only just turned the knob on my front door. It was too late to escape.

"Good morning Mr. Taylor."

"Earwood," I grumbled as polite a response as I could muster after my evening's adventures.

Howard Earwood was a bane of my existence. Ok that might have been an overstatement but he was definitely a bane of someone's existence. Earwood was a minister, and I used the term loosely, of the so called non-denominational Wings of Spirit church. Two streets over in a small church that looked more like a cross between a barn and an ice cream pallor with a bright glowing neon sign out front, proclaiming salvation every Sunday. It was nestled among residential homes and I thanked God everyday, which I should have anyway, that it wasn't and he wasn't my neighbor.

"The church is having a revival this Sunday, Mr. Taylor. You're very welcome to come . . ." he positively chirped.

I turned around, my battered face greeting him.

"Oh . . ." Howard half exclaimed dropping the glossy flyer he was holding out.

I knew I looked bad, but maybe this was one benefit of being beaten up. It might repel Earwood's evangelical advances.

"What happened? Was it gangs? I've seen gangs around here . . . a robbery?" he adjusted the suspenders he always seemed to wear of his almost Amish clothing. His non-existent lips seeming to disappear even more as he asked.

I was tempted to say Presbyterians but I didn't. "Broken window," I finally replied again not completely a lie.

Howard looked at my old brick building with distain, like it was a death trap to the surrounding community and should be torn down. I could have told him it was Nazis. I should have told him it was Nazis, but something told me Howard's deeper moral convictions might not have a problem with Nazis as much as Presbyterians or myself and my old brick house.

"Mr. Delmar was asking about your church the other day . . ." I began. It wasn't a lie. I'd heard Mr. Delmar cursing something about a flyer he'd found in his mailbox.

"He was?" Howard returned, the smell of a potential new recruit in such close proximity lacing the early morning air.

"I think he's out on his porch actually . . ." I offered.

"Oh well . . ." Howard presented me with one of the glossy flyers. "Sunday . . . you're welcome to come. I think you could use some God in your life," Howard smiled and started down the sidewalk.

If he only knew . . . I waited until I heard him approach Mr. Delmar on his porch.

"Keep your damn religion to yourself you whiney bible thumper . . ." Mr. Delmar barked from his porch even before Earwood got a foot near the house.

I couldn't help a chuckle as I stepped inside my front door. It was an ornery thing but I needed a laugh. My old building seemed happy to see me, but still sleepy from the early hour. I had the sense she opened an eye, relieved to see me then rolled back over to catch a few more winks.

After double checking the lock on my front door, tossing Howard's glossy flyer in the trash bin and reasoning I needed a little bit better security on my office front and maybe my whole building. I dropped my bag at my desk, noting the spare eyeglass case Mr. Zalbowski had left behind, and pushed through the curtains. I headed straight for the kitchen. I was famished. I know, I know crisis, people to save, but I hadn't eaten in forever. I wasn't saving anyone on an empty stomach. Besides it was a waiting game now, waiting for what I didn't know.

I grabbed a few chicken breasts, out of the fridge I had thawed, and threw them in the skillet with some butter. Opened the fridge again and pulled out an arm full of fresh veg, I had only just gotten from Tabitha at Hollow Tree Farm.

I should call the hospitals check on Brandon if I could find him.

But first I'd eat. Tabitha would approve. I wasn't going to be good to anyone if I didn't give myself some fuel.

After a good meal and a cold shower, since I'd still forgotten to turn on my heat pump, I examined the now purple ugly bruises tattooing my torso. I reasoned they would probably very soon have new friends and covered them with some clean clothes, a gray t-shirt and some blue jeans. Next I headed downstairs to check on things. The timers on the lighting and fans were working fine. I added some water and nutrients to the reservoir for the plants. Opened my small workspace lab to double check an experiment I had running which seemed well adjusted and in no need of immediate attention.

Then I stopped at the old unplugged fridge against the bricks of the basement wall. I hesitated. I slid its empty carcass out on a special hinge I had constructed. Behind it hidden from view was a large iron door, with a great levered lock. I hesitated once again. If I used what was behind that door people would know it was loose in the world again. But, I reasoned I was going up against something unknown, with four possibly five lives that needed to be saved. I was only one man. I could use every help I could get. It wasn't like it hadn't been used before in similar dire circumstances. Like the chaotic circumstances that had brought me to the future, I stared immobile at the large iron door. I also told myself it wouldn't work for everyone there was some reassurance in that, right. But in the back of my mind I heard, yeah sure, it only takes one dark person with the power to wield it and then what. I hesitated. There was a reason I hadn't used it in thirteen years; well if you count time travel more like sixty-three years. I had used it the last time because I had lost someone and look at what had happened to me.

My thoughts turned to Tabitha and the twins, to Mr. Zalbowski and his missing son. If God had made it for any reason . . . if it was meant to ever be used . . . it was for reasons like this. I took hold of the great iron lever and was about to pull it up when I heard the bell on my front door sound. Still grasping the lever I waited. The bell rang again. I let go of the iron lever and relocked the padlock. I swung the dead fridge back in place and headed up the stairs. My decision would have to wait.

CHAPTER THIRTEEN

The pull bell sounded once again just as I passed through the curtains. I could see Joseph peering through the window of the front door, his fingers combing through his coif of dark hair. When he saw me coming he did a short wave and stepped back from the door.

"Joseph," I said opening the door to him.

"I wondered if you got back, then I saw your car . . . what happened?"

I didn't ask him if he'd walked all the way over. It was obvious he had. He was sweating slightly from the warming heat of the morning sun.

"So what happened? Did you find the boy? See any Nazis?" he questioned with a wry chuckle, strolling across my office. I noted he had one of Earwood's flyers in his hand that was half crumpled. Howard had accosted him on the way over.

I shrugged and walked back toward the living room leaving the curtains open to the office; where Joseph had stopped to lean against my desk.

"What? What happened?" Joseph questioned a pitch of worry now entering his voice as he quickly followed me, since I hadn't answered a single question with my dropped shoulders. "Where's Mr. Zalbowski?"

"They took him and they took my friends too," I grunted, dropping to a chair.

Joseph seemed stunned as he sat down on the sofa across from me. Slowly I told him what had happened after he'd left yesterday, about the Forrester's and my less then stellar idea to use Hollow Tree Farm as a safe haven for Mr. Zalbowski. I also told him about Dr. Cox and Leoda Pharmaceuticals. How they had let me go, when they could have trimmed me like one of their well manicured hedges, only probably bloodier and with more holes. I told him about Brandon, who had ended up bloody and beaten no thanks to me, and the rendezvous appointment with the unknown orchestrator of this whole chaotic affair, which now apparently involved myself quite deeply even though I didn't know how or why. I finished with the ultimatum I'd been given. Apple. Sunset.

"What are you going to do?" Joseph asked once he had recovered his ability to speak and was staring at me from his seat on the sofa.

"Go . . . of course," I returned. "I don't have a choice."

"You don't even know who it is or how many there will be . . . you're *sure* you can't call the police . . . ?" he grimaced with hope.

"Nazis," I returned with snark.

"Still?"

"Joseph."

"What if . . . whoever he is . . . he just wants to tie up loose ends and you're a loose end . . . and he's already taken care of the

Forrester's and Mr. Zalbowski . . . and you're all that's left . . . and he figures why go to all the trouble of finding you when you can come to him . . ." Joseph shrugged.

"Really . . . laziness that's your reasoning?" I questioned.

"I don't know," he returned appearing a bit rattled, his voice rising.

"That's reassuring Joseph."

"Well it might be true," he shrugged again.

"Then why leave Brandon alive . . . heck why leave me alive or let me go for that matter and why meet him at Apple," I hadn't told Joseph the whole reason for Apple either . . . and what it meant personally to me. Telling him would have caused me to veer into a territory of many more questions. Questions when already he was having enough trouble with the plausibility of Nazis in Iowa. Trust me my story would cause bigger questions.

"Why this Apple? You said it's in Illinois? I've never heard of it. Why Illinois, when we know they're in Iowa. I don't get it?" His eyes were honest and they looked at me with sincere question. See I told you one fact only leads to more questions.

"They chose Apple because of me."

"You?"

"Yeah it . . . it means something to me," I try really hard to limit my lying. Why . . . because I'm a terrible liar. When I say terrible I don't mean I'm bad, I mean I'm horrible. There are many times I have endangered my own life because I can not tell a lie. Not that I don't want to, mind you, I just can't. So I stick to omission, omission is a lie right. Well it turns out I'm not all that good at it either. But I'm a hell of a lot better at omission than lying, only thing is omission usually catches up with you. They say lying does too, I wouldn't know I get caught before I've even finished the lie most times.

"What? What does it mean?" Joseph queried.

"Something personal," I answered trying to give him a tone that meant don't tread any farther than you need to.

Joseph shifted uncomfortably in his seat. His eyes glancing questioningly to my bulletproof curtains probably wondering just who exactly I was. "But if it's personal . . ." he started needing some clarity but not pushing.

"Whoever it is they're trying to throw me off my game," I answered.

"Haven't they already done that . . ."

I gave him a cynical expression.

"But why?" he continued. "Why do something so elaborate? Why kidnap Jeffrey Zalbowski if they were after you . . . why him, you didn't even know him. I mean that doesn't make any sense . . . if I hadn't told you about him . . ." Joseph frowned.

"I don't know . . ." I admitted, which pretty much encompassed everything. This was a longer term game than I was use to playing. Though there was a connection . . . the connection was Leoda and the war. The war had given birth to Leoda and it had formed my future as well . . . events after the war had brought me here . . . to the future. "I need to find out if Brandon is alright . . ." I said, Joseph's questions of loose ends had caused me to worry if maybe he was right. I needed to know Brandon was safe. Not just a no show at the hospital or DOA.

"I can get Tanya to find him," Joseph offered.

"Tanya?" I questioned.

"My assistant."

"Your secretary?" I raised an eyebrow.

"I refer to her as my assistant," Joseph returned a bit indignant.

"I'm sure you do," I smirked.

"Do you want her to find him or not?" Joseph questioned with a dark look.

"Ok," I answered and Joseph walked into my office to use the phone. I had maybe four hours now to plan before I had to leave for Apple. I didn't know what the hell I was going to face. I thought about what was hidden downstairs. I mulled it over for a few seconds. I made my decision. It had rested idle behind that empty old fridge and that iron gate for too long. I was going to use the blasted thing. Using it would be worth it if it meant saving peoples lives. I needed to save their lives. I wasn't losing anyone else. Yes, I would use it.

"Ok," Joseph said returning. "She'll call back when she finds out anything."

"So Tanya . . ." I smarted looking at him.

"Don't you have other things you should be focused on?" Joseph sputtered, his cheeks flushing.

"You're right. We can deal with your lack of love life later."

"*My lack* . . ." Joseph laughed.

"I don't suppose I could borrow your SUV?" I innocently questioned with a small smile.

Joseph got suddenly very serious. "You just wrecked my car yesterday."

"Technically that was you," I generously pointed out.

"What happened to your car last night?"

"Rogue mail box, metal post . . . . the usual."

"Usual?" Joseph scoffed.

I was glad I didn't tell him about the armed guards, tall fence and the moat . . . who has a moat in the middle of an Iowa cornfield anyway. "I need the room. I might need to get a lot of people out of there fast," I returned.

"Not by yourself . . . not with my car," he returned determined.

"You're not coming with me."

"You want my car. You get my help. Besides you need a driver . . . a get away man," Joseph said patting his chest proudly.

"This isn't a bank robbery Joseph."

"I know that," he answered.

I had insulted him again. I seemed to be really good at that.

☙❧

I hadn't yet accepted Joseph's demanding offer when the bell on the office door rang once again. Joseph and I both looked past the curtains to the clear glass of my office door. Miss Haptonstall stood at the window, a pair of dark sunglasses obscuring her eyes.

"Miss Haptonstall," Joseph responded with a note of delight.

"What about Tanya?" I snarked moving toward the door to let her inside.

"Funny," Joseph returned with an irritated and guilty tone, crossing his arms as he sat back down on the sofa.

"Miss Haptonstall, what are you doing here?" I questioned leaning on the open door, but not allowing her entry.

"Is that any way to greet your employee," her tone was crisp and I wasn't sure if she was being condescending or sarcastic. So I opened the door and made a gracious gesture for her to enter.

"If there's a problem with our understanding that working at home actually involves working at home I'd be happy to clarify," I began.

She slapped a manila file folder at my chest and I quickly grabbed it before it hit the floor.

"I'm not here for you . . ." she replied. "I'm here for Mr. Zalbowski . . . ." she hesitated. "I felt sorry I had to leave yesterday." Her tone was suddenly softer now as she looked around the house. "Where is Mr. Zalbowski?"

I grimaced.

"This ought to be good," I heard Joseph grumble from the living room.

"Why? What happened?" Emily questioned, turning to me with a focused almost accusing tone.

"Why would you think anything happened?" I responded.

Emily took off her sunglasses and narrowed her steely blue eyes at me. I felt suddenly like I was about to be scolded for something.

"Because I've known you all of three days . . . . and if the previous two were any example then there's no doubt the third will be the same."

I had to give her that. She wasn't running away like most people would have done in this situation. I didn't know if that was to her credit or not. I mean I knew Joseph was crazy. He was my friend. It seemed to be a prerequisite for anyone who got to know me. What with kidnappings, robberies, beatings and Nazis; most sensible people would be heading for the hills. But here she was at the doorstep of the fray with a file folder and sunglasses, looking quite refreshing to my battered eyes.

I heard Joseph laughing in the other room. "Wait till you're here a whole week," he called.

"So what is this?" I said holding up the manila folder and ignoring Joseph's vocal comment from the living room.

"I did a little extra checking into Oxfam Chemicals and Leoda Pharmaceuticals . . . as well as Mr. Zalbowski and his parents."

I opened the folder and pulled out a neatly categorized stack of papers. They were divided into two sets. The cover papers read Oxfam, Leoda and Zalbowski. There must have been fifty pages.

I looked back at her. "So what does it say?" I inquired, not having the want or time to sit down and read through them all.

"Which do you want first," she said walking into the living room, acknowledging Joseph and casually taking a seat. She seemed quite at ease making herself comfortable in my house. The confidence reminded me of someone else I'd known, so did the cheek.

I smiled, looked down at the ream of papers and followed her into my living room. It wasn't about Zalbowski or at least I didn't believe it was.

"Oxfam and Leoda," I replied figuring I already knew quite a bit about them, but even the smallest thing might help me now.

"Well," she leaned forward, intent and earnest. "Oxfam, of course is a subsidiary of Leoda but they've got some very interesting connections . . . government connections . . ." she gave me a pointed look.

I took a seat next to Joseph on the sofa, already consumed by the passion in her voice, and the information . . . of course the information.

"Connections to the Department of Energy and the Department

of Defense . . . they seemed to be primarily involved in research and development. But they also have major side company connections to agriculture, communications and telecom companies, bio-engineering and hybridization programs. All things which if you take the Nazis eugenics hypothesis . . . fits quite neatly into a slow progression of ideas . . . twisted ideas but . . ." she paused.

"You know Nazis they like things neat and well recorded . . ." Joseph injected with a grimacing snark. He was hoping sarcasm was enough to maintain his current state of deluded bravery . . . overlooking Nazis, pharmaceutical companies and kidnappings, staying focused on just helping Mel.

"I thought you said you didn't believe the whole Nazis in Iowa premise?" I questioned, looking back at her. She ignored me and continued speaking. I didn't take offense most people did that anyway.

"Now Leoda Pharmaceuticals is a whole different story . . . they're a major manufacturer of eleven of the top US selling drugs and six of the world's top selling ones. They say their headquarters is in New York State but they own property everywhere. Lots in South and Central America, in fact just last year they took over two of the largest pharmaceutical producers that were owned by South American companies . . . and they have large European holdings as well. They have enormous legislative power here and abroad and their lobbies have had a dramatic impact on different bills that have been before Congress and the Senate. Odd bills to . . . like security and finance bills . . . nothing that I could see that had anything to do with pharmaceutical companies," she paused as though she was still trying to see exactly how those pieces fit into the others. "One other thing . . . that location you had on your map . . . they don't just own that . . ." she stood up taking the stack of papers from beside me. She thumbed through them momentarily until she came to a map. It showed the state of Iowa. "Every dot represents some property or business under their ownership . . ." she presented it back before us with an indicating finger.

There had to be thirty-five to fifty dots most in major cities but many lay in the middle of nowhere. I handed the map to Joseph. Who examined it intensely, as though his mind was recording everything.

"And that's just Iowa," Emily continued. Her voice filled with intelligent discovery. "There are other states with even larger numbers . . . and these are just under the heading of Leoda not the fifty or sixty other companies Leoda owns . . . they're literally *everywhere* . . ." she stopped and looked at me as if expecting me to explain everything she had discovered into a far broader understandable context somehow.

I leaned back. I wasn't surprised but obviously Miss Haptonstall had been able to glean a great deal more from the internet than I had researching in libraries and public records. She was definitely going to be an asset. She was thorough too, to note I had only identified about half of Leoda's holdings, of course I hadn't been solely focused on them. The information appeared quite shocking to her as her expression revealed its still startled horror over the paper ramifications of what she had learned.

"What about the current owners?" I questioned other more personal concerns on the forefront of my mind.

She frowned. "That was something odd . . ." she leaned back in the old leather chair where she was sitting across from us. ". . . openly they state they only have a board of directors and no CEO. Which could be possible but their whole system is designed as if there's a head honcho. I even came across a memo stating something to that affect," she pointed to the papers again. "I contacted a friend of mine and she said financially a large chuck of money is not going to the board members . . . though apparently they've done a real good job trying to hide it, but you know the IRS. They follow the money . . . they brought Capone down . . . she said there has to be someone at the top. There's just no way of finding out what his name is. The only thing she could find was from when the company originally formed in 1948 . . . but nothing more current."

1948 . . . I thought but didn't say anything.

"That still doesn't completely explain why they wanted Zalbowski or you for that matter," Joseph said. "I mean they had to be following Zalbowski's family from the war, when his father was in the camps. How on earth would they keep track of them like that . . . they were defeated . . . weren't they, the Nazis . . . and I mean the possibility of Zalbowski's father dying or not having any children . . . or it's huge . . ."

I knew a lot more than what I'd told Joseph or what Miss Haptonstall had learned; for instance my own connections to far less public events during and after the war, especially in 1948. I held my tongue.

"What does he mean, they wanted *you*?" Emily asked with a heightened tone, her blue eyes questioning me.

I quickly filled her in on the past evening's events, with Joseph adding the perhaps unneeded snide comment as I went.

"And you have no idea who it could be?" she questioned. "Who you're suppose to meet? Who took Mr. Zalbowski or your friends?"

I shook my head. It was true I didn't know. I had inklings but then nothing I could come up with that had any certainty which probably meant my worst fears would be true. That was the kind of thing that usually happened to me. I pulled out my silver pocket watch to give it a wind and check the time. It was nearly noon a few more hours and I still didn't have a plan. Joseph noted my observance of the hour.

"When do we have to leave?" he asked.

"Not till at least three," I returned.

"*We?*" Emily asked. "You're going with him?" she turned to Joseph with a note of surprise . . . and maybe worry.

Joseph nodded and gave her a shy smile, his fingers brushing through his hair and giving it an unneeded lift. "I'd better go check in at the office . . . get my car . . . and see if Tanya found anything out about Mr. Forrester. I'll be back before three," he said stepping over my feet and leaving through the front door of the office. I glanced back at Emily had she scared him off by showing such concern.

"Don't you think you should call the police?" Emily said, looking back at me after Joseph's departure.

"And tell them what 'Some Nazis have kidnapped my friends . . . do you mind getting them back for me . . . they're supposed to meet me at sunset in a non-existent town . . .'"

"I'm sure they've heard stranger things."

"I'm not in the mood to get arrested . . . or put my friends lives in the hands of strangers even if they do have a badge . . . maybe especially because they have a badge."

She shrugged. "What will you do? You can't expect to just ask them and they say sorry it was all a mistake."

"I planned on saying pretty please."

"It's not funny."

"Sometimes funny is all you have left," I replied.

"But your just a genealogist . . . what can you do?" she questioned. I noted a tone that added . . . what do you even know how to do . . . I was however a lot more than that but I held my tongue. Omission remember.

"I can do my best . . ." I softly replied.

"But these are people's lives," her voice revealed her worry.

"I think I know that . . . they're my friends . . . ." I paused and looked down at the stack of papers. "Thank you for this . . . you didn't have to . . ."

"It was for Mr. Zalbowski," she returned, looking away from me for a moment.

"Did you make your appointment?" I asked, hoping she'd look at me again with her blue eyes.

"My appointment?" she questioned, turning back.

"The one you left for . . ."

"Oh yes . . . yes. It was fine," she replied leaning back in the chair. Her blue eyes returning to look out the front window, then finally back at me. "You will be careful . . . you did just hire me . . ."

"Worried about your job?" I half smiled.

"Worried about my boss . . . who employs me . . ."

"Worried about your job," I repeated with a raised eyebrow. It was strange. I felt comfortable around her. I didn't find myself trying to impress her or present myself as anything else. I felt as though I could honestly say just about anything to her. "So Miss Haptonstall . . ."

"Emily please," she offered softly.

"Emily," I returned with a small smile. "Have you lived here all your life?"

She nodded.

"So . . . Haptonstall that's an unusual name . . ." I couldn't help myself. Ever since she told me her name I'd been wondering, could she be related to the same Haptonstall I had known. I couldn't help my eyes wondering about her body . . . looking for similarities of course. "There can't be that many families with that name around . . . I mean . . ."

"Oh I didn't tell you what I found about Mr. Zalbowski," she suddenly said as though she was desperate to change the subject.

"Mr. Zalbowski . . . . right . . ." I returned, perhaps it was best to leave the past buried.

"His father, you know was in the concentration camps but so was his mother . . . a different camp. I couldn't find any more information on her . . . but hospital records in Wisconsin show that when Mr. Zalbowski was born his mother became violently ill," Emily said handing me what looked like a hospital form.

"You found this on the internet?" I questioned in disbelief.

She looked at me with her steely blue eyes and smiled. "I have my ways . . ."

I raised my eyebrows. Oh she was definitely a Haptonstall.

". . . anyway she nearly died," Emily continued.

I grimaced.

"They had no more children, only Mr. Zalbowski . . . a year later she died . . . it was reported as heart failure . . ."

"He said his own wife died in child birth . . ." I started.

"Yes, I thought the same thing . . . odd coincidence . . . ." she paused, a sad cadence in her voice. "Interesting note or just extremely weird . . . like Kennedy assassination weird . . . the name of the doctor that delivered Mr. Zalbowski is the same as the name of the doctor that delivered Jeffrey his son . . ."

"What?" I questioned.

"I told you it was weird. I checked twice. The exact same name. First and last," she shuffled some of the papers.

"What was the name?"

"Lewis T. Cox."

"Cox?" I blurted out, my face going ashen.

"Do you know it?"

"Leoda Pharmaceuticals, last night the skinny guy in the expensive suit. They called him Dr. Cox . . . but there was no way that guy was old enough to have delivered Mr. Zalbowski. Mr. Zalbowski's in his what . . . late forties or early fifties . . ."

"Forty-six," Emily corrected, apparently memorizing her research was another talent.

"This guy I saw last night was my age give or take five years." Still I thought as I said it, you should talk. You were born in 1916.

"Family maybe?" Emily offered.

"Maybe," I mumbled.

"Still that . . . well that's just weird . . . isn't it?" she peered at me again expectantly as if I had more to tell her.

"Welcome to my life . . . weird to me is getting to be blasé. The last two days haven't been exactly normal," I returned. Then again maybe this was normal.

"That's good to know . . ." Emily said with a soft smile.

"Yeah," I answered with a chuckle and checked my watch again, giving the wind not even a single turn. I should eat something again before going, or not, yeah and I needed to get stuff together. Joseph needed to get back. I hoped Brandon was ok and I needed to go back downstairs. I needed to prepare myself. I was taking it. I had decided. I looked across at Emily. There was a long period of silence between us.

"You probably have a lot to do," Emily began noticing I had pulled out my watch once more and was checking it for the second time.

"No . . . I just, I'm anxious . . ." I lied, well partly I was anxious. She hesitated.

I really did stink at lying. For a moment I almost felt like she was going to ask to come along, then she stood put on her sunglasses and turned to me.

"Take care of yourself Mr. Taylor," she offered with an almost business tone.

"Melburn," I returned, common curiosity.

"Melburn," she repeated a bit softer.

I couldn't see her steely blue eyes through the dark glasses and I missed them.

"Be careful."

"I am, it's mostly just other people," I said making a sad joke.

The front door opened with a clank of bells chiming. Joseph had returned.

"And take care of Joseph," she said walking past him to the door. Joseph nodded with a smile.

"I will and don't worry . . . you'll still have your job tomorrow . . ." I said as she slipped out the door.

"You're supposed to take care of me?" Joseph questioned, wandering into the living room.

"She's worried about you," I returned.

"She is? Did she say that?" Joseph looked at the door, half expecting to catch another glimpse of Emily.

"Did Tanya find out anything?" I questioned, somewhat delighted to watch Joseph squirm every time I mentioned her.

"Yeah . . . she ah . . ." he turned away from the door. "She found him, Brandon Forrester . . . Mercy Hospital, room 314. He's out of critical and stable. He had two broken ribs, two cracked ones and a broken arm . . . and a fractured ankle," Joseph said ticking off the list of injuries on his fingers. "The guy was in pretty bad shape when they got him to the hospital. Apparently the police were out to the house and interviewed Mr. Forrester in the hospital. He said it was a home invasion, meth addicts . . . and that his family was luckily out of town . . ."

I felt bad about having Brandon lie, but for everyone's sake, including the police it was probably safer.

"Look I need to get some things together. Why don't you fix yourself some food. There's some chicken breasts cooked in the fridge."

"Should I . . ." Joseph hesitated. "Should I bring anything?"

"Just your SUV," I returned.

"Outside in the drive, full tank of gas."

"Good," I said walking into my office and grabbing my old leather bag. I locked the front door, handed Joseph my bag for a minute while I closed the curtains then took it back. "Now go make yourself some food I'll be downstairs."

Chapter Fourteen

I could hear jars and silverware clanking as I walked down the stairs. The floor boards creaked overhead as I heard Joseph wandering about in the kitchen. Soon I was back at the empty old fridge. I took a deep breath and swung the fridge out once again, revealing the large iron door and locking lever.

Taking hold of the combination lock, a few quick spins and the new lock opened. I breathed out. I had made my decision. There was no turning back now. With a rather grating grasp I pulled the lever out of place and swung the heavy door open. The small brick walled passageway was tiny. No more than a closet really, its doubled solid brick walls without a single window or opening save the large iron door. The smell that greeted me was musty from lack of air circulation. The hole held the odor of the exhaling bricks that formed the space and lingered in the shadowed darkness, as slowly it inhaled fresh air from the now open doorway. Had someone closed it I could only shudder at the coffin like claustrophobia. The light of the basement shown in enough to find the dusty metal loop handle sunk into the floor. Sticking my fingers through the metal circle I gave a hefty heave and got my other hand under the lip of the cement slab that matched the rest of the floor perfectly.

The slab had two metal pins that hinged like a colossal heavy trap door. Below at the bottom of the recessed square hole was a simple wooden box. It was long and skinny and felt cold against my hands from its long interred rest in the ground. Looking at it you would never suspect anything of great significance or value lay inside. You would be wrong. Inside that plain dark stained and weathered oak box was perhaps an item of the greatest power ever known to man. It had come into my possession more than half a century ago. The last time I had used it, I had regretted it. Not for what it did but for what it had allowed me to do. I had lost more than my sanity in the taste for revenge that day, I had lost my friend.

I hadn't held it in my hands since. I opened the lid. An undecorated white fabric covered the contents. I licked my lips and lifted the white covering. There it was, deceptive in its inactive appearance, a dull sort of brownish-gray that darted in dull flashes in the shadowed light. It was about eighteen inches long, perhaps one and a half to two inches in diameter. Along the dull shaft were dark, almost charcoal black etchings that appeared to be carved along the staff's face. The lettering or characters were obscure, ancient. Its origin was in a time that history had forgotten or rewritten. To a skilled eye single letters and glyphic runes could be identified or at least associated with ancient Hebraic or Egyptian but they were so different that even to the trained eye the letters and words were deceptive. They were meant to be. They had not been written for all to read.

At a distance it looked like nothing more than a rather large, thick stick. Both ends of the shaft however ended in six sided points like a crystal and to the inexperienced which end was which was difficult to determine.

I however had held the rod before and knew how to wield its strength. I reached forward; before my skin had even touched the shaft it iridesceed in a swirling pale bluish light. It sensed me. Grasping hold there was a distinct vibration, something akin to a musical cord being struck and an electric current coming on emanated in the air around me. Whether this feeling was from myself or the staff I was uncertain. The staff iridesceed again only brighter. This time it began to radiate off a cool bluish glow almost like a fog filling the air about me. The longer I held it the clearer the staff became until its heart shone like a white crystal. The carved letters and glyphs burned with a white intensity that was nearly blinding at their heart. My hand felt no heat from the glowing light which hovered about me in vortexing clouds of pearlized sapphire illumination. It had remembered me and I it.

I held it there a moment longer, feeling the raw power flowing in me, around me. Tapping points in the universe like pin pricks along my skin. Then as quickly as it had activated I closed my eyes and the staff returned to its dull hidden appearance. Hastily I wrapped it in the same white cloth from its box and set it aside; while I replaced the wooden box and closed the cement slab with its now empty chamber. I picked up the covered rod and stepped from the brick coffin closet, swinging the iron door shut and dropping the lever with a banging solid thud. I didn't bother to lock the combination, but swung the camouflaging old fridge back in sentry.

My old wide mouthed leather bag would have to serve as its sanctuary for the time being. The sapphire staff, an instrument of divine power that could wield the forces of heaven and earth was now going to ride shotgun with me while I attempted to save my friends. It was an instrument of God's will, I was just hoping his will was with me tonight.

✪✪

I wasn't sure how long I had been downstairs, but it had been long enough for Joseph to have finished eating. He was still sitting at the table, and had a satisfied look on his face. A large empty plate sat in front of him.

"I was about ready to come and find you," Joseph said folding one foot over the other and stretching out on my chair.

I sat my bag down on the table and pulled out my watch. It was after two. I had been in the basement for over an hour and a half. I had experienced this before when holding the staff without any other distraction you could easily blend into a trance like harmony.

"So did you get everything you needed?" Joseph questioned tapping my bag.

"Yeah," I answered, moving the leather bag to the counter and started to fix myself something to eat from what Joseph had left. I had no idea what was going to happen, and I wanted as much energy as I could muster. "Look," I began making myself a sandwich. "I don't want you getting out of the car unless I tell you to, if anything, for any reason goes wrong . . . I don't want you to hesitate . . . get the hell out of there."

"You mean just leave you?" Joseph returned with question.

"I mean save yourself. This could go colossally wrong . . . I don't know what to expect . . . like you said it could all just be a trap to get me."

"But?" Joseph began sitting up in a more serious and less relaxed position. "How will I know . . ."

"I trust you," I returned. I highly doubted he'd need much explanation as to what colossally bad could mean. He'd been around me enough to know.

Joseph didn't say anything. He had a quizzical look on his face, half way between sickness and confusion. It was a look I often had on my own face.

"But," I began. "I'll try to get Tabitha, the twins . . . Mr. Zalbowski and maybe his son . . . so if you have to leave me . . . I'll be ok with that . . ."

Joseph swallowed, telling him he might be responsible for more people hadn't helped easy his worries. His face veered more into the sick expression rapidly abandoning its confusion.

"Joseph it's still ok . . . you can back out. You don't owe me or any of us anything."

"I got you and Mr. Zalbowski involved. I was responsible for that . . ." he said with pointed emphasize.

"If whoever's doing this wanted me and Mr. Zalbowski to meet . . . it was going to happen with or without you. Besides I have a feeling Mr. Zalbowski and myself have been in these people's radar for quite some time," I said sitting down at the table to eat my sandwich. My small attempt to elate Joseph's fears didn't seem to be helping as I munched at my food. "Now," I said hoping to get

Joseph's mind on something perhaps, anything different. "Your assistant Tanya . . . which one is she . . . not the little short woman with the blonde perm?"

"No . . . that's Mrs. Robinson," Joseph gawfed. He stopped and gave me a look like he knew what I was trying to do, changing the subject. He seemed to appreciate it and proceeded. "She's the one with the curvy red hair . . . her name's Tanya Kelley."

"And what will Miss Haptonstall think?"

"Why? Did she say something?" his face lighting up.

I chuckled and took a big bite out of my sandwich. There was no way I was answering that one right away.

CHAPTER FIFTEEN

We were on the road by four. Mr. Delmar saw us off with a glowering stare and maybe a snarl. I was driving as I knew the way south. Back country roads didn't change much even in seventy years. We would stop before getting close to Apple and Joseph would drive us in. He asked me how I knew where we were going, especially if Apple wasn't even a town anymore. How would we know where to find them. But I knew exactly where we would meet them. The place where the answer to history was time. The place where my history had begun.

I didn't expect the farm house or the barn to be there. If there was anything left it would most likely be derelict and abandoned. A former shell of what I remembered, very much like everything from my past. I had missed fifty years of the world skipping over them like a flat stone on water. Now I was coming home.

Memories are a funny thing. They make places and people survive long beyond the pale of history and time; even after the minute ticks on a clock have eaten away with eroding forces all that once made those memories solid. I knew what I remembered wasn't what existed now, but in my mind they did. The same as they had when I had last seen them. Maybe existence was just a collective thought . . . a tuning fork struck by consciousness . . . if it is, I only wondered what are we thinking.

It had been seventy five years since I had been home. I call it home, but my two story brick dinosaur was more a home than that farm had ever been. Maybe once it was, but I couldn't remember those distant days. I had been twenty years old when I last saw the place. I was now only forty-four and yet it had been seventy-five long years. Still I wasn't prepared to see home. I had worked my way through college then joined the army when the war department basically didn't give me a choice. I had seen the beginning of the war and I had seen the end of the war. I had seen the world change and I saw the world today with a cynicism I never believed I could have had as a child. That was not until my brother Sanford's death. It was a death, not a suicide like so many believed. I had proved it even if no one believed me, or cared. It was the last time I was home. The last time I had stepped foot in Apple.

I had been full of arrogance and purpose. Wanting so much to prove Sanford, my brother, had not died by his own hands. That he had been forced, forced by circumstances beyond his control. At the time I believed it, fresh from the proving grounds of academia. I was a fool. But I had needed a reason, any reason to blame them for Sanford's death, my parents. They had taken a sweet innocent boy and placed him among people in white coats that rightfully should have been clothed as undertakers. There had been nothing wrong with Sanford except a soul far more sensitive to the world, than society could understand. I could understand their fear now.

I had seen so much more . . . those ranting words, my pompous bravado . . . I wished I could have left things better. But they were gone now just as Sanford was, just as so many were. I was still here and I was coming full circle, back to Apple.

Now something or someone was drawing me back. I had been back in the Midwest now for almost two years, after nearly eleven years of slow reestablishment, readjustment and sadness elsewhere. My circumstances were due in no small part to my sudden jump into the future or hurtling as the case may be, I mean it's not everyday when you skip from 1948 to 1998. It takes a period of acclimation. It takes a minute just to figure out what's going on. What things are, and that first year had been hell. Things that had been just theoretical were now an every day occurrence. So much history had passed me by. On top of everything I had developed my new unique physiology of being able to destroy just about any electrical appliance I came in contact with. Let me tell you that was a fun learning experience, especially in an age that was ruled by electronics. It had finally been hearing about the Forrester's missing twins that had pulled me back to the Midwest. I questioned now, knowing the little I knew, if it too had been orchestrated. A lure placed in the water to bring me in, by whoever was controlling these current events. If the twins kidnapping was . . . it had worked.

The landscape was starting to get familiar, or maybe I was just anxious. But we were close enough. The sun was riding low in the sky, playing at the tips of the corn and the gentle flat rolling hills where the brush and oak trees obscured the horizon. I pulled over to the side of the gravel road.

"Your turn," I said to Joseph and opened the door of the SUV. I was impressed other than the clock continually flashing 12:00, the SUV was still running. My electric dysfunction was boding well. I was hoping it would continue. You know hope, the eternal optimist.

Joseph quickly followed suit and we switched places. I had given Joseph my gun. He said he knew how to use it, but I showed him anyway. I wouldn't need it. I had the sapphire staff. Luckily the temperature was dropping with the sun. The humidity of the past few days was ebbing, but there was still a late summer heat that hung in the air refusing to give up. I grabbed my army jacket, an old style one the guy at the surplus store had told me, it wasn't old to me. The flat collar, the color, it was very much like the one I had been issued. Well except for the few modifications I had made. I picked up my leather bag and placed it on my lap.

"Turn here," I said as we came to a small white and black rural route marker. Joseph complied. The road dove and crested, up and down for the next mile or so before leveling out. We were getting close. I opened my bag and pulled out the long wrapped staff, dropping the bag between my feet. I unwrapped the staff and slowly slid it down a specially designed pocket on the inside of my jacket.

"What's that?" Joseph questioned, his knuckles tightening and loosening on the steering wheel.

"Insurance," I returned.

"Don't you have a gun or something . . ." his voice was anxious and worried. ". . . don't tell me you just have a big stick . . . you're not Jackie Chan . . ."

"Who?"

Joseph grumped as he flipped on the headlights.

"Don't worry . . . it's not a stick," I replied. The sun was falling now deep behind the horizon and trees. A few bright rays sending orange and purple ribbons streaking across the sky as the day's candle snuffed out in blue gray puffs of clouds.

"Then what is it?"

"Headlights," a deep voice called from the shadows surrounding the old farm house.

Cox paused and took a calm step to his left. He looked past the broken glass of the rotting window frame, toward the distant deserted country road. He could just make out the faint movement of the vehicle's form in the fading light. "Finally . . ." Cox said. He turned back to his occupying business. He cleared his throat and waved his hand. The bruiser dropped Mr. Zalbowski back to the floor, his legs crumpling beneath him.

"My son . . ." Zalbowski sputtered once again exhausted and breathing heavy. It was the only words he had uttered in hours. It was the only thing that mattered, not his safety or his life, only his son. Cox had tired of his wasted time and useless efforts. They had reaped nothing of use.

"Replace the gag . . . and leave him," Cox barked.

The large man who had been assisting Cox by beating Mr. Zalbowski's blindfolded and bound body, shoved the cloth gag back in the damaged man's bloody mouth and tied it tight.

Cox straightened his suit. "He knows nothing," he said with a note of failed disgust. He paused to watch Zalbowski momentarily struggle on the broken dirty floor boards. "It seemed not worth the effort," he sighed and sniffed to himself. He hadn't completely agreed with this tactic or this rather theatrical dance to draw the players together. He looked once more out the front window frame at the cautiously approaching SUV. "The woman first . . . and remember what you were told about the man . . ." Cox nodded indicating Zalbowski to the large bruiser who now had his gun in hand.

The bruiser nodded in silence and trained his weapon toward the broken window.

ᘒᘐ

"Turn in at that big evergreen," I indicated ahead of us as Joseph's headlights illuminated the dense tall pine. "And keep your eyes open."

We didn't have to look far, as we came down the lane toward the old farmstead. Four black SUVs were parked near the front of the collapsing house. They made Joseph's SUV look puny by their steroidal comparison. As for the house and I use the term loosely. Half the roof had collapsed inside the structure. The windows were broken or missing. Areas of the white siding where the headlights of our car struck showed peeling paint and rotting wood. They were right you can't go home again. But there was still a sad note of nostalgia, of something that had once been a part of me, now lost.

"That's far enough," I told Joseph. "I don't want you getting any closer." I stayed in my seat waiting, watching the shadows closer as the sun fell completely from the sky leaving everything in darkness, until only our headlights illuminated the front of the house.

Then as if just realizing he had visitors, Dr. Cox appeared on the front step out of the shadows.

"That's Cox," I said wiping a bead of sweat from the top of my lip. I could hear Joseph swallow hard. He reached for the keys preparing to shut off the engine. "Don't," I growled. "Every second counts . . ." That and I didn't trust the car to restart with me in such close proximity with the sapphire staff.

Joseph took his hand away, his fingers returning to their white knuckled grip on the steering wheel.

"Well here goes," I said taking hold of the door handle. I opened the door. The whooshing change from the stale air conditioned environment of Joseph's car to the warmer night with its living smells of grasses, earth and faint manure, hit my nose and senses, which were already open and alert.

"Mr. Taylor, so nice of you to come," Cox welcomed with a cordial greeting.

"I'm here," I bluntly replied.

"So you are."

"You and I already had our conversation Cox. I didn't come to speak to underlings . . . so don't waste my time."

Cox's congeniality dropped away, replaced by a vicious hateful leer.

"Now if your boss or whatever isn't here why don't you just give me the people I came for and we can all call it a night. You can get back to suit pressing or whatever you do for fun," I noticed he had on another expensive charcoal suit. Italian probably, they were always Italian.

"Brave words for someone in such a position."

Movement in my periphery caused me to look away from Cox. I counted at least six men, all about the same size. Like moving walls they started to surround me, three on either side lurking in the shadows. They were staying out of the beams of the headlights where I was standing. But their feet were softly kicking up dirt into the shafts of the light.

"Well it's pretty cowardly of your boss to invite me to this party and then be a no show. How am I suppose to take that . . . almost makes me want to leave without saying goodbye," I snarked.

"Then where would your friends be," Cox returned.

"As far as I can see my friends aren't here."

Cox signaled to someone in the shadows of the house. From the darkness came a sprawling figure, who hit the ground hard sending up a cloud of dust before me in the headlights.

It was Tabitha. She was gagged and blindfolded. Her hands tied tightly behind her back. As far as I could tell she wasn't hurt severally, maybe some scraps and bruises but nothing that wouldn't heal. I held my ground, never once faining weakness by wanting to help her. To these people Tabitha and the others were expendable, nothing more than bargaining chips.

"That's just one . . . there should be four more . . ." I said thankful she was alive.

At the sound of my voice Tabitha rooted around finding me. Even through the muffled garbled sounds I knew she was calling to me. She had no idea I could see her.

"Greedy aren't we?" Cox replied. His calm knowing demeanor had returned.

"Maybe," I answered. "So Cox," I put a little extra emphasis on the x. My hands were sweating and I could only hope I wasn't sweating so much it could be seen through my jacket. I fought to keep my voice steady, my eyes monitoring Tabitha on the ground, who was inching toward the sound of my voice. Smart woman. "What's it like to do your boss's dirty work. I say boss because I know you're not in charge. I just don't see it. If you wanted me you could have had me the other night. But no," I pointed at him making sure to do it quickly so he wouldn't see my hand shaking. "You let me go why . . . because someone told you to . . . and now here I am and still nothing . . . didn't get your orders today?"

Cox laughed.

Ok that wasn't the reaction I was hoping for, but maybe I could win him over with humor.

"To think such a pathetic little man could have such power . . ." Cox shook his head.

"Thanks . . . I think . . ." And who was he calling little . . . I was taller than he was. Focus. I needed something to set him off balance, anything. "Lewis T. Cox . . ." I started drawing his attention directly at me. "You've been busy delivering children haven't you . . ."

Cox laughed again.

Again not the effect I was looking for. "Mr. Zalbowski . . ." I started.

"You have no idea do you . . ." Cox returned. "I tire of this game . . ." he spoke to the shadows behind him. "Let us have done with it . . ."

"You never did have patience, Lewis," a voice said in the void of black beyond the headlights.

I squinted trying to make out whoever it was.

"Mr. Taylor or should I say Captain Taylor . . ." A six foot tall man with perfectly styled hair and an immaculate light gray double breasted suit stepped out of the darkness. The light reflected off his tiny spectacles flashing at my eyes, causing me to blink. I looked back to make sure it wasn't an illusion. It wasn't. He was exactly as I remembered him.

"Delgado!"

In one swift efficient movement he bowed his head and clicked his heels. It sent a chill through me.

"Surprised Captain Taylor."

It took me a minute to respond. I tried to keep my mouth from gaping in astonishment and fear, I didn't do so well. My mind was racing with questions and screaming with danger. A situation that had looked impossible had just gotten so much worse. I steadied myself, once again looking at Tabitha. Her struggling form in the high beams of the car as small puffs of dry dust floated tan particles about her. The exhaust smell from Joseph's SUV wafted forward on the breeze, stirring me back into the urgency of my rapidly deteriorating situation. I needed to regain a footing. I had to be smart. I had to be bold. How the hell was I going to do that . . .

"So . . ." I began my throat as dry as the dusty ground I was standing on. "Delgado all this for some great theatrical reveal . . . to show me someone who should have died sixty years ago, is still alive . . . I'd be surprised . . . maybe even impressed if I didn't see that in the mirror every morning . . ."

"Really Mr. Taylor . . . no curiosity . . . no questions about how . . ." his words lingered in the night air.

"You know that's the problem with people like you. You can't just do something evil and be satisfied . . . no . . . you've got to make sure everybody knows . . . that it was you that did the big evil thing."

"Perhaps . . . a little glory is due to the geniuses of history."

"Genius?" I scoffed. "You think highly of yourself . . ."

"Then please Mr. Taylor enlighten us about your vast knowledge."

I had forgotten how much I hated this guy's voice. That slinky German accent that wasn't quite right, it had that weird undertone of some other language maybe Spanish or Portuguese or something South American.

"There was only one device Delgado and I destroyed it. That's what caused me to be sucked through time . . . obviously you were close enough to be sucked through too . . ."

Delgado scoffed with a slight chuckle.

It was my best guess. I didn't know how the damn device had worked. I was trying to destroy it. How the hell I had survived and gotten thrown forward fifty years was a big enough mystery. So if Delgado didn't show up next to me when I'd landed in that field in the future; how was I to know he hadn't landed somewhere else. God this guy was getting on my last nerve and it was already stretched to the limit. The smug pompous . . .

"Look," I said "This walk down memory lane is great but I didn't like you all that much when I knew you before . . . so let's call it a nice reunion. You give me my people and I'll meet you in the next fifty years or so . . ."

"You are right about one thing," Delgado began, motioning to Cox. Who had stepped back. "I was there the night you destroyed the device. Just as I was there when you tried to stop Dr. Eunholder from testing the device the very first time. You were lucky on both instances, Captain. But tonight there are no little Jewish doctors to save your life . . ." he smiled.

My lips twitched with a snarl. My sweaty hands rolled into fists. My eyes lowered and I held Delgado in a dark stare. I was angry now, angrier than I had been in a very long time. I could feel it coursing through me like waves of heat. If it hadn't been for the people I was trying to rescue I would have killed him there on the spot without a regret or sense of guilt, like I should have done years ago, but somehow some inner force held me from acting.

"What you and your little dead Jew never realized was that Dr. Eunholder had constructed two devices . . ." he waited for the impact of his statement to sink in. "Yes two . . . and while you may have put a temporary misstep in my efforts by killing Dr. Eunholder. I obtained . . ." he smiled with a self assured arrogance. ". . . help with the necessary insights to perfect the device and further my research . . ."

"So all this," I said through gritted teeth. ". . . for your Reich, for the glory of the master race . . . sorry to tell you but the war ended . . . all your efforts to continue on failed . . ."

"I have never failed . . . the Reich had its purpose Captain Taylor . . . but the Reich was never our goal. It was an experiment like so many others . . ."

"And me . . . and my friends?" I spit.

"Don't think of yourself so highly Captain Taylor . . . as for the Zalbowski family they have always had greater connections to my goals than you do . . . and they have been a research project of mine for far longer than you know . . . you were but . . . the icing on the cake . . ."

"Why all this then? Why the kidnappings? Why the ruse? Why me?" I questioned. My hands still gripped in tight fists.

"So that I would have something you want," Delgado replied.

"I don't . . ."

"Understand . . ." he interrupted. "Captain Taylor . . . it doesn't surprise me. You had *it* with you the night you destroyed the first device . . . I could hardly believe my fortune . . . a weapon that wielded such power. A weapon to rule with, to control with . . ." His expression was ravenous. The light flashing like reflectant orbs off his spectacles. "An object by all rights that belongs to me . . ."

I suddenly realized what everything had been about . . . getting me to come out in the open, drawing me back to a familiar setting with the twins. Allowing me to think I could have a life. Then Zalbowski and his son, all of it, everything so I would be willing to use it . . . to reveal it and if at all possible trade it for my friends lives. The sapphire staff.

"I think he may understand . . ." Delgado said with a broad smile.

I glanced up with a startled expression.

"You have been a thorn in my time Mr. Taylor."

I could hear Cox's snickering laugh in the shadows.

"You have evaded me . . . and tried to destroy what was mine . . . not for much longer . . ." Suddenly Mr. Zalbowski was thrown into the dust with Tabitha, wetting my appetite no doubt. His rumpled suit jacket was gone and the white dress shirt was untucked and spotted with blood, no doubt his own, from the marks I could see even on his blindfolded and gagged face. "The sapphire staff Captain Taylor and you get your friends . . . your life . . . everything that you want . . ."

"What makes you think I have the staff?" I returned.

"Captain Taylor do not insult me. I know that you have it and I know that you more than likely have it on your person . . . at this very moment . . . in fact in a way I am sure of it . . . if you do not you are more of a fool than I thought you were."

God I wish I were more of a fool. "Give me all my friends and I'll give you the staff," I started.

"Do you take me for a fool also, Captain Taylor."

I wasn't sure how to answer that one. "Do I have to answer that one . . ." I swallowed. I breathed out a jittery breath. What the hell was I going to do now. "I haven't seen the kids yet . . ." I added either bravely or stupidly.

"And you won't until we have a deal . . ."

"Ok . . . let me get these two out of here . . . you show me the kids . . ." I licked my lips. "I give you the staff."

"No . . . take them, give me the staff and you get to live."

"Kids or there's no deal," I said standing my ground like I actually meant it. Which I did, because I couldn't have been lying at least it sounded an awful lot like I believed what I'd just said. "If you've waited this long what's a few more seconds . . ." I bravely barked back.

"Or I just kill you now," Delgado declared. Two large dark shadowed behemoths pointed their weapons at me.

Now was the time to be bold or brave or both. "You know that won't work not if I have the staff."

"Has it ever been attempted at this close a range, without you holding the active staff," Delgado questioned with a calm that was unnerving.

He had a point. Crap. I didn't even know if the kids were here or alive. With Tabitha and Mr. Zalbowski at my feet it was too much of a risk to chance anything yet. But I had to make sure the kids were here.

"Go ahead," I said in my bravest tone. "Give it a try." Please, please don't let him call my bluff.

Delgado paused a moment, then gave the ever so slightest nod to Cox. Half a minute later three young boys were dragged onto the dilapidated porch.

I swallowed trying to keep the dryness from over taking my mouth.

"Ok they go in the car first," I gestured to Tabitha and Mr. Zalbowski.

Delgado nodded. He had no intention of killing Zalbowski or the boy . . . not yet anyway.

What was bothering me was why he hadn't just already shot me. Why was he letting me get Zalbowski and Tabitha? I mean if Delgado thought I wasn't protected by the sapphire staff why not just shoot me and everyone else then just take it. Really that's what's bothering you . . . why the evil Nazi bastard hasn't shot you already . . . focus . . . save the people . . . you can worry about him killing you later.

I waved to Joseph to come forward. His SUV crept slowly closer. The seconds ticked by taking an eternity. The shifting tires and the crickets were about the only things audible. Finally when Joseph practically had the bumper against my legs, he got out of the car. I was still waving at him, my eyes never leaving Delgado for a second.

"Get them in the car," I said under my breath.

Joseph ripped the blindfold off Mr. Zalbowski and helped him to his feet, grabbing Tabitha's arm at the same time and getting her to her feet. He was half way back to the car when he pulled off Tabitha's blindfold and shoved them both in the back seat without a word. His door closed and he backed the car off a few feet.

"Your turn Mr. Taylor . . . the staff," Delgado voiced.

Oh . . . I took a long calm breath out. This is where it was going to get bad.

CHAPTER SIXTEEN

I started to reach into my jacket.

"Wait!" Delgado shouted.

I paused, my hand not yet inside my jacket. I couldn't hear or see all the armed men but I knew every single weapon was trained on me.

He gestured to one of his bulky shadow gunmen. The man approached me. He was another brick wall like the last one. I was beginning to think there was a catalogue these guys were ordered from. Buy five get the sixth one free.

Tiny reached in my jacket with all the finesse of a bear looking for a hidden ham. He ripped at the fabric, pawing me like a piece of meat. Then he felt it and pulled it from the clothed sheath of my jacket.

"Here," he grunted holding up the unimpressive brown gray stick. Delgado had just enough time to smile.

"Thanks tiny," I said grasping the correct end in my hand. The intense flash of blue white light hit the brick wall with a wave of force sending him skittering back through a broken window into the house with a shattering hit. The entire structure shagged. The sapphire staff glowed with a clear righteous crystal intensity. The glyphs hot white against the cool etheric blue.

The gunmen opened fire. Bullets ripped through the night air toward me. I crouched down intensifying the cool blue swirling field until it surrounded me. As long as I kept it burning so intensely the bullets wouldn't strike me. I heard the engine of Joseph's SUV roar into reverse as bullets ricocheted off its metal sides. Two gunmen had taken the incentive to turn Joseph's vehicle into Swiss cheese.

I whirled on the two gunmen and sent out a sudden shock of blinding light. A great crackling bolt of blue lightening shot out from the end of the staff. It arced in the air painting horizontal bolts of lightening that etched the black night. Its powerful beam shot right through one of the gunmen's solid forms and out the other side. I whipped around not waiting to see what happened and struck the other gunman with a crackling lash from the sapphire staff.

Joseph's SUV was still moving. It hit the hump in the camel backed county road with a jostling leap. Joseph had gunned the accelerator so hard he careened backwards across the road and took out several yards of the adjacent cornfield.

I turned back to the house. The remaining four gunmen had recovered from the blinding flash of light. Their bullets ripped through the warm night air toward me. I wasn't sure exactly how the sapphire staff stopped them. It wasn't like a shield, the bullet pinged off. It was more like they disintegrated from matter back into the very essence of energy they had been formed from.

"Kill them!"

I heard Cox give the command, pointing to the children as he and Delgado moved away from the fray.

"NO!" I let out a cry outstretching my arm with the sapphire staff. A blazing blue struck the gunman closest to the children. The force was so great it looked more like he had been sucked through the tattered house rather than blown through it, his gun coughing out stray bullets as he went. They stabbed the boards of the porch perilously close to the children, who clutched at the dry rotted wood for protection. I could only hope none of them had been hit. Cox and Delgado took off in a run around the house into the darkness.

One of the gunmen took the unfortunate incentive to tackle me while my back was turned. One thing about the staff, it can protect you from bullets, even grenades but some brave or stupid soul decides to tackle you while your back is turned. It's not going to warn you. It's also not going to save you.

I hit the dry ground, my chin smacking the dusty earth with the sudden impact. I still had the sapphire staff in my hand, but the behemoth got in a few really good cracks to my ribs and torso, several right where I was etched with preexisting welts. I puffed out, pulling the staff in closer to my body. He grabbed at the staff half expecting I think to rip it from my grasp and become employee of the week. He was wrong. When the sapphire staff scorched his eyes with its holy fire the look of shocked terrified surprise was evident for about half a second before he was thrown thirty feet into the dark air.

The three remaining gunmen continued to fire their weapons. Rolling over I glanced to the porch. The light from the staff was illuminating most of the surroundings in a luminescent azure hue while the stray flashes of gunfire did the rest. The children were still on the porch huddled together against the boards, their hands and arms clutching at each other in terror. I could make out the blonde hair of the twins that appeared almost white in the light of the staff, as well as one dark haired kid, Jeffrey Zalbowski.

Two of the gunmen however were keeping their attention firmly directed at me stalking closer and closer, as I struggled to my feet. The holy sapphire light was still about me, protecting me from their bullets. I had lost the third one. I checked the kids. He wasn't there. Then I felt it. A piercing burning pain ripped through my back and torso. I dropped to my knees on the ground with a yell. The third gunman had taken an example from the earlier successful tackle. Only this one had brought a knife. He pulled the blade back with a vicious slash. Its sharp edge slicing out of the jagged wound he had just caused. I cried out but didn't loosen my hold on the staff, protecting myself from the continuing gunfire at my front. The behemoth raised his knife preparing to bring it down like a dagger into my back. I looked to the children. I couldn't be stopped here. I made the effort to turn. Hoping I could grab the dagger with my other hand before it struck.

I barely grabbed his arm in time. I fell backwards onto the ground. I felt the pain from my back as I hit the earth, striking hard as if it was a second blade. I released my grip on the staff to defend myself from the stabbing dagger coming down at my head, dropping us all into darkness save for the pale moonlight, now obscured by clouds. He jabbed at my wounded side with his fist. I yelped out in pain. The knife struck the earth next to my head as I dodged. He jabbed again a bloody smack to my bleeding torso. Ripples of pain shot through my body like white hot needles. My senses screamed.

The blade came at me again. The darkness of night had surrounded us as the sapphire staff lay quiet on the dusty ground beside our death struggle.

I didn't hear gunfire now no doubt the other two gunmen were as blind as we were. The clouds shifted and I saw the dagger above me. Its sharp brilliant metal was alight now in motion. Then out of the darkness a single bullet shot. Its path struck the gunman's head as he brought the dagger down at my chest. The bullet passed through the man's head in an explosive exit of the gunman's face. The blunted bullet impacted the ground ahead of me with a puff of swallowed dust, missing me by only inches. The gunman slumped, his bloody mass toppling onto me.

It was Joseph. My gun in his hand as the dead gunman landed next to me on the ground.

"Mel?" Joseph yelled.

We didn't have time. The last gunmen had become shadows in the dark. They opened fire again, randomly and unaimed but still deathly dangerous. I grunted trying to move, trying to find the staff, trying to get out from under the dead behemoth who'd fallen half on top of me.

Suddenly the sapphire staff burst to iridescing life. Joseph had found it. His hand wrapped around it. His face illuminated in shock. I didn't have time to be shocked. I was in pain and bleeding and the kids were still cowering on the porch. Gunfire exploded once again against the blue billowing circle that now engulfed Joseph.

"Use it like a shield," I barked, struggling to rise.

Even though Joseph didn't know what to do, he shut his eyes and held the staff horizontally in the air, his hand grasping the center of

181

the staff's length. Blue lightening shot from either end of the rod, cutting quickly through multiple layers of metal to finally consume two of the black SUVs on either side of us. The two cars exploded in giant orange balls of fire, sending thundering instantaneous lights into the dark sky.

"Shit!" Joseph cried falling on his rump next to me on the ground. Smoke billowed from the two SUVs burning carcasses, as gasoline ignited in concussive blasts scattering broken fragments into the air as projectiles. "What is this thing?" he questioned, still enveloped in the sapphire swirls of the unknown holy fire.

In the flashes of orange and blue, I saw my gun on the ground where Joseph had dropped it. I grabbed it. The solid metal of the old pistol was heavy compared to the balanced ephemeral weight of the staff.

"Don't ask questions," I yelled. "Just get the kids out of here." I stood up aimed at the first gunman I saw and fired. The bullet struck him square in the chest, which would have been perfect had he not been wearing Kevlar. Crap.

I shot again this time aiming for his leg. I missed.

He coughed off a blast of bullets in my direction. Luckily Joseph stepped in front of me, the blue shield absorbing their deadly intention. They became harmless ripples on the etheric pond.

"Stop playing around. Get the kids," I pushed him toward the porch. The moment he moved I shot again, this time striking my target. The gunman went down with a crying yell. I'd struck his knee and upper arm.

Joseph was at the porch, when more bullets ripped past me from the darkness. I aimed wildly and fired twice. More bullets coughed out of the darkness in flashes of light. I aimed high at the flashes and shot twice more. The muscles of my back were crying at me to stop, but I couldn't, not yet. I heard a thump and then nothing. One of my bullets had struck.

One of the burning SUVs exploded with a loud outward blast, sending more flames and smoke into the dark starry sky. Tongues of fire now licked at the edges of the dry rotted wood of what remained of the old farm house, quickly consuming its desiccated forlorn carcass.

Joseph had the children. The twins clutching to his side and who I could only assume was Jeffrey in his arms. The headlights of Joseph's SUV were coming toward us. Either Zalbowski or Tabitha was coming to our aid. The sapphire staff was now lifeless in Joseph's hand as he carried the children toward me. Who would have thought of all people, Joseph. The sapphire staff worked for Joseph.

I fell to my knees. "Get them out of here," I barked with a contorted snarl of pain, pointing toward the approaching car. "I'm going after Delgado."

"Mel are you crazy?" Joseph yelled in disbelief.

"You have to ask that," I returned surprising even myself with the cognition for a come back. I could feel the blood running down my back, warm and wet. I was starting to feel chilled but I knew Delgado couldn't have gotten far. I wasn't going to let the bastard get away. Not this time, not a second time. They had run like his kind always did. I pulled myself to my feet and headed in the direction they had run.

"Delgado!" I roared rounding the old house that was fighting desperately against the hungry flames. An exploding tire from one of the SUVs made a huge blasting noise. "Delgado!" I cried running out farther into the empty field.

Then suddenly I saw Cox's pasty white skin in the moonlight. His gun trained on me. I pointed my weapon not realizing the pain that would ripple through my body on lifting it. We stood there momentarily, the acid smoke from the burning cars filling the night air. Popping explosions of what was left of tires and internal structures slowly being eaten away by the consuming flames.

"Captain Taylor," Delgado came out from behind Cox.

"Delgado," I felt my arm and shoulder contracting. My body trying to protect itself from the harm I was doing to it, but I never lowered my weapon.

"You continue to be a thorn in my side."

"Glad to oblige," I returned my arm shaking as I held the gun.

"I was hoping for a better outcome . . . this time . . ." Delgado voiced.

"So was I," I replied. "Now I shoot you and Dr. Cox and I'm done."

"How wrong you are," Delgado returned. "Shooting me will only continue this game . . ."

Cox didn't move. The chance of me killing them both was impossible so I aimed for Delgado. I had at best one maybe two bullets left. At least I could save the world from him. A faint beeping sound went off in Delgado's suit.

"I'm afraid Captain Taylor we will have to continue this conversation at another time," Delgado pulled a small five inch bulbous black circular clock looking device from his side pocket. He calmly observed the series of rotating dials under its glass covered face.

It was one of Dr. Eunholder's devices like the one I had destroyed more than sixty years ago. My eyes and face betrayed my fear and shock over the sight of such a small innocuous looking instrument. Dear God, I thought I had destroyed it.

"Yes Captain a working prototype. You see unlike yourself I am not confined to the randomness of time," Delgado opened the face of the device, seeming unconcerned by my pointed weapon. "You have no idea what you have trespassed upon or what you will suffer because of it."

I could shoot him now, but then Cox would shoot me and the device would still be useable. Cox could use it. Delgado pressed down on the device's lever. The air shimmered about him.

"Didn't you wonder why I called this meeting for after sunset in a certain location Captain . . ." Delgado began.

"You found the windows!" I returned aghast at what that single piece of information could mean. The gun was shaking in my screaming grasp.

"Ja," Delgado smiled and took a step back. "We will be seeing you Captain, auf wiedersehen."

My aim for Delgado was at his heart, if the bastard even had one. At the last second I aimed for the device and fired. The bullet struck the device in Delgado's hand, just as the air about them started to change to a warm glow of honey light.

"You fool," Delgado declared with a shake of his head. His voice was low and almost calm. Its steady timber frightened me more than if he had screamed. I knew what came next. When a device of Dr. Eunholder's was damaged or destroyed in the act of functioning. It was like being at the center of an atomic bomb.

The silence was consuming, then the sensation of heat against your skin. The blinding light until you and everything collapsed into the darkness.

As Cox and Delgado were sucked somewhere in time I was thrown up and backward hurtling hundreds of feet through the dark air. For a split second I was weightless among the sparkling stars of heaven, celestial pearls on a dark sea of tranquil sapphire wonder. It didn't last. I didn't feel myself hit the ground or hear the screaming cries of agony that left my mouth and crippled my flesh. I didn't taste the blood trickling from my mouth onto the dry earth. I only hoped I had destroyed the device and imprisoned Delgado and Cox in the time they were meant to be in. The past, where their danger and deeds were already done.

⁌⁍

"Mel? Mel?" Joseph was trying to rouse me. I couldn't feel his insistence to get some response from me but strangely though, I sensed it. I sensed my own body but not with feeling or touch but some other worldly tethering that held me to whatever I was, from some far distance.

I wanted to tell him to stop. Let me sleep, leave me alone, but he continued until I was annoyed by his jostling efforts; until out of my mouth came a guttural growl and a whimpering mumble.

"Help me get him to the car," Joseph barked.

I felt arms dragging me. I smelled rubber and gasoline tinged with bitter smoke that cut at my throat and stung my nostrils. I wanted them to put me down. I wanted to go to sleep. I was cold and tired. The pain was there. It hadn't left. But it too seemed distant, anesthetized by my own unwilling consciousness.

Orange flames flashed in my periphery. Then I felt shoving hands and the pain returned. It shot through my back in flashes of blinding horror. Twisting knots that warped and gripped about my body's frame till my muscles convulsed in excruciating agony. The curved edge of the car door rubbed into my face. I could hear voices, but they melded into my own moaning whimpers.

"Oh God is he alive?"

"He's breathing . . . he's alive . . ."

"Mel?"

"He's bleeding everywhere."

"We have to do something."

"What?"

"We need to get him to a hospital."

I made a mumbling gasping effort to answer. To say not to take me to a hospital, but my friends took my efforts as more cries of pain; which it partly was and felt the need was even more urgent.

"I'll do what I can," it was Tabitha's voice.

I felt force and heat against the wound. My head was sliding back and forth on whatever surface I was sprawled upon. I didn't have the strength to steady myself against the car's motion. I blacked out recalling Joseph's voice. It was raised at a high pitch and nervous, but strangely commanding. Making sure everyone knew what they were doing and were doing it.

Chapter Seventeen

I don't know how long I was out but the next thing I remember was someone pulling at my shoulders. The painful yank traveled down my back like a wake up alarm. I groaned loudly in pain.

"Come on Mel," it was Joseph. "We're almost there."

Joseph was shorter and thinner than me and from the manhandling way he was jostling me around he wasn't doing a very good job hanging on to me.

"Stay in the car," he ordered. Then I felt my feet dragging across cement and I could hear Joseph's strained effort in his wheezing breath.

I heard the whoosh of automatic doors and the cold brush of circulating air against my already chilled body. My eyes fluttered noticing a white tiled floor beneath our feet.

"I need some help!" Joseph's heightened voice called out.

Suddenly I was in the air and moving quickly. Voices were talking in rapid half understood words, fingers poking and prodding at me.

I tried to say something, but I was thrust onto my side. My jacket and clothes were being cut away. Not my jacket, I liked my jacket.

"What happened?"

"Car accident," Joseph lied, but he lied better than I did.

"Come on," the doctor returned.

Ok, maybe he didn't lie better than I did.

"This is a knife wound. Nurse get him out of here," the doctor ordered.

My eyes fluttered I was becoming more aware. My body had been thrashed a hundred different ways over the years so I wasn't surprised I was beginning to come around. Nurses and doctors, people in brightly colored smocks bustled about in all directions. I felt needles prick the skin of my arm and the flesh about my back. I heard the continued conversation of assessing my condition and what was needed. This was not going to be good. I opened my eyes again wider. "Don't . . ." I mumbled. "Don . . ."

"Wait what's wrong with this thing?" a nurse fretted. "This can't be . . . it says his blood pressure is 4000."

"Get another on," someone ordered.

"His pulse says . . . 600, no 75 . . ."

It was too late. You see there's one other thing. The reason I don't live in a building with lots of modern electronics like computers and such . . . is partly because being transported from the past to the future by a Nazi time machine that you just tried to destroy with a grenade while being protected by the sapphire staff and blowing yourself up . . . . well apparently it messes you up electrically . . . harmonies and all that . . . maybe God wasn't planning on grenades and Nazi time machines and suicide attempts when he handed the staff out. Or maybe he was. Basically I could short out, malfunction and blow up just about any device or electrical system. Put simply . . . I make things go boom. It had gotten better in the thirteen years since the incident but I hadn't used the sapphire staff in thirteen years either. Tonight I'd not only used it I'd also destroyed another of Dr. Eunholder's devices. More I was coming to, this hospital was in one hell of a position for a major power outage.

"What the hell?" another doctor growled as more and more equipment began to malfunction.

Lights started flickering in the ceiling. Monitors and beepers all over the floor started sounding their alarms. The lights fritzed once or twice before dropping everything into darkness. Emergency generators kicked on, in seconds, but even the restored power hadn't slowed the chaos down. Machines and computers were spitting flickering sparks. Nurses and doctors were in a panic to check on what was and wasn't an emergency. Voices quickly raised into a ruckus of commotion. Soon the emergency lights started popping and shutting off. An old doctor walked into my curtained theatre looked at the stunned nurse holding the gauze packed against my wound. It seemed everyone had abandoned her and me in the uproar. He grabbed an emergency flashlight and sat down at my bedside and started barking orders. The other people in scrubs snapped to attention and immediately started following his orders. The flashlight flickered and fritzed but maintained an almost dull brown orange glow. A few minutes later after I had been cleaned and prepared, the old doctor started suturing. He seemed oblivious to the chaos, while he attended my knife wound. I was almost alert but the area around the wound had been chemically numbed, so I didn't feel much as he stitched my sundered flesh. He reminded me of other doctors during the war. I had seen one doctor continue working without pause when a bomb blew out half a wall only five feet from him. He had covered the patient one minute and returned to finishing his surgery the next.

I was weak but conscious when the doctor finished me up. He barked something at the nurse then moved like a calm center out into the maelstrom of the ringing, beeping and yelling emergency room. The nurse finished her orders regarding me and soon exited into the chaos with the others. I was all alone. A minute later in my curtained haven someone touched my shoulder.

"Mel?"

"Joseph," I looked up from my collapsed, abandoned position. He was still here.

"Hey."

"We need to get out of here," I said immediately, trying unsuccessfully to move, let alone sit up.

"Are you kidding, you're in no shape . . . I was just going to tell you I was taking the others home . . . the nurse wanted me to fill out your paperwork but the computers started smoking . . ."

"Someone should tell them it's bad for their health," I mumbled rolling over to my good side. They'd given me something to numb me . . . it was half working.

"Funny," Joseph said flinching as what sounded like a cart full of metal bedpans hit the floor somewhere in the chaos. I don't know why there are always bedpans, but there's always something that sounds like them.

"I need to get out of here," I repeated grabbing Joseph's partly blood stained shirt and pulling myself up with his help. I grabbed a little more desperately as pains from unnumbed areas screamed at me. "Get me a wheelchair and shirt . . ."

Mine was in ribbons on the floor, soaking in blood along with my jacket.

Joseph stared at me a moment with wide eyed apprehension. He didn't argue. He wasn't about to after everything else that had happened tonight. He steadied me on the bed then slipped behind the curtain again disappearing for about five to ten minutes. The chaos was continuing and somewhere in the storm I could hear a woman screaming and doctors barking at nurses, as electronics buzzed and sparked. Alarms of all sorts were blaring and squawking in every direction.

Joseph returned with a wheelchair and a sickly green scrub shirt. I slipped it on and nearly passed out again from the pain.

"You're sure about this?" Joseph questioned, trying to assist me.

"This hospital isn't going to find any peace until I get out of here," I replied easing into the wheelchair and leaning forward away from my back with Joseph's help.

There wasn't a lot of need to be clandestine about sneaking out. It was at a point in the chaos where the staff would have been grateful if everyone had left. So we were out in the parking lot before anyone was the wiser. Joseph rolled me across the black cement to his waiting SUV in minutes. The sun hadn't risen yet but darkness no longer held a firm grip on the sky.

My only hope was that his car would start with me inside it. Joseph helped me up and inside. I was breathing heavily by the time

I was in the front seat. Mr. Zalbowski and Tabitha were still in the back seat bruised and battered. A strange sort of stillness held the car, parents cradling their rescued children, exhausted, frightened children who now sat in unconscious protection on and in the laps of hugging embraces.

Joseph climbed in and turned the key.

The SUV shuddered and coughed. It idled with a jittering sort of uncertain heartbeat but it kept going. It drove forward in stuttered jerking starts and I realized this was the third car of Joseph's that had been totaled. If it got us home it would be a miracle. His repair bills alone since he'd met me had to have sky rocketed along with his insurance. I really needed to pay him back. We pulled out of the hospital parking lot. The clock in the dashboard was now blinking off and on 12:34, 12:34. I'd have shaken my head at the shear insanity of it but I just closed my eyes.

☙❧

When I awoke next the car was stopped and I found myself staring at a brick wall. It was red brick like my own brick wall. I couldn't be sure if it was home. It still wasn't dawn and I was alone. I wasn't sure what had happened or where I was, perhaps the car had quit. Maybe Joseph had just left me not knowing what to do.

A second later the car door opened with a pronounced squeak and Joseph was standing there with Mr. Zalbowski. My eyes opened but that didn't seem to matter to them.

"Take his arm . . ." I heard Joseph say but between the two of them not much more crossed their lips.

I was barely conscious and all I could think was I hoped they didn't drop me. As the two men pulled me out of the car I recognized my house. We were back. Tabitha was holding my solid steel back door open as they carried me inside. I lolled a half understandable thank you at Tabitha as I was hauled through the doorway.

I watched my feet as they dragged me along the dark tiled stone of my kitchen, then bumped my feet over the lip onto the wooden floor of my living room and finally down the short carpeted hallway to the rugged nap of my bedroom.

I remember hitting the soft sheets of my bed. There was a play of lights in the distance with mumbled voices that I couldn't understand and didn't want to and then nothing, not another thing.

CHAPTER EIGHTEEN

I awoke to the sound of dishes and children playing. And for a moment I thought it was a dream, a beautiful wonderful dream of warm breakfasts and families, of farms and brothers, of innocence and love. Then I moved and the evening's events crashed back into my memory and body. Oh God was I sore. Every part of me hollered at what I had done. I couldn't apologize they were yelling too loud. I moved slowly hoping the blood would assuage their thirst. It didn't. I had fallen asleep on my back and the tight drawing stitches were singing a dirge of misery.

I groaned heartily as I made a greater effort to move. I sunk back down in the bed deciding rising might not be the best idea.

"Good morning." The voice was sunshine.

I opened my eyes to find Tabitha standing at the foot of my bed.

"Morning," I rasped in return not realizing how dry my voice was.

"Let me get you some water," she exited the room, quickly returning a few seconds later.

I rose slightly trying not to groan as I did so. I did anyway. After finishing a couple of gulps Tabitha placed the glass on the small table across from my bed and I leaned gratefully back in bed.

"Thank you," she began, brushing a ribbon of blonde hair from her eyes. ". . . for saving my boys again and for me . . . and my husband . . ."

"Brandon?" I questioned, my eyes finding her.

"I talked with him this morning. He's back home already and probably doing things he shouldn't be doing," she said picking up some clothes from my floor and placing them in an already overburdened chair in the corner. "The boys are fine too . . ." she gave a small thankful smile.

"Mr. Zalbowski?" I questioned.

"In your upstairs bedroom still asleep. His son next to him."

I breathed a small sigh of relief. Things could have turned out a lot worse.

"I'm not exactly sure what happened, and I'm not sure right now I want to know," Tabitha started, a relieved look on her face. A darkening bruise held the edge of her right cheek just above a nasty scrape of scabbed, healing skin on her jaw. "The important thing is we all survived and we're all safe."

We should be I thought remembering what had happened to Delgado and Cox. Crap, Delgado had been alive . . . had he been in the future as long as I had . . . or longer . . . he'd had a working device . . . what had he been able to do in all that time . . . but I had shot it . . . I had destroyed it last night . . . at least I sure as hell hoped I had.

If Dr. Eunholder's device had worked, or rather had malfunctioned like it had with me, when I'd destroyed the first one then they'd ended up in a field somewhere in the middle of nowhere. Obviously I'd destroyed one of Dr. Eunholder's devices in 1948. I remembered the explosion. Hell I dreamed it. I relived it. What I hadn't known . . . what none of us knew . . . was that according to Delgado . . . Dr. Eunholder had made another. All I could hope was that the one I'd shot, last night, had been the last one; the last of Dr. Eunholder's little temporal corruptions. If Delgado had been aiming for home . . . for the past . . . sixty or so years ago when I shot the device, that was where Delgado ended up. I could pray that with hope, luck or whatever else I could muster he had been stranded there, rightly dead by now. That was unless he figured out how to make another of Dr. Eunholder's devices. Hope and luck however might not be enough because that wasn't what was frightening me the most. I know you'd think evil Nazi doctor scientist on the loose with a time device would be enough . . . nope.

The most frightening thing Delgado had said was he had figured out the windows, the windows of time. Windows were places, temporal moments, that with the right key could allow you to access time like a hallway full of doors. At least that was Dr. Eunholder's theory. Dr. Eunholder hadn't yet figured out an accurate method of calculating the windows before I destroyed the first device in 1948. But if Delgado had perfected the calculations for the windows and reinvented the device . . . I couldn't help a gulp . . . but I thought Delgado would already have done it wouldn't he . . . if . . . I mean . . . if he went back sixty some years . . . he'd had time to try again but . . . I looked around no Delgado . . . at least that I knew. I felt suddenly dizzy and confused. God this time stuff made my head hurt.

"Melburn?" Tabitha repeated with question as I pondered my growing headache.

"Sorry," I said breaking away from my thoughts.

"You need your rest . . . I'll stay until Joseph comes back . . . my brother is coming to pick up me and the boys. There's food ready to eat in the fridge and I baked that apple pie you got the other day. You need your rest . . . make sure you do," she smiled softly.

"Thanks mom," I returned. She patted my leg through the bed covers before leaving. I realized for the first time I was only wearing boxers. At some point someone had striped me. I lifted the blanket and looked down. My chest was a patchwork of bruises and injuries. With the bruising scratch lines and the pummeled fist marks it looked as though someone had used me to play tick-tack-toe with knuckle rings.

I lay there a few minutes longer then decided to chance a trip to the bathroom. It wasn't that far away. They say the first step is the hardest. I'd change that to the first twenty and then the twenty back.

I took a couple concoctions of my own making, which helped to dull the pain after a few minutes but it wasn't letting me forget. Grabbing my flannel robe I felt the tight pull of my back muscles and proceeded gingerly to the living room.

"Mel!" Joseph was sitting in one of my old leather chairs, in clean clothes. He'd apparently been to his home and back. His feet were propped up on the foot stool. He was the apparent babysitter of my condition.

I looked around slowly no sign of Tabitha and the twins.

"She just left," Joseph returned.

"Good she shouldn't have waited. I'm sure Brandon can't wait to see her."

"She called him last night and again this morning . . . found out he was home. They talked for about an hour," Joseph said. "I think she went over every second . . . twice."

"And you?" I ever so gingerly descended onto the sofa with a groan.

Joseph breathed out and leaned back in the chair. "I can't say I haven't got a lot of questions because I do . . . like who the hell are you and who were those people and what is that thing? . . . with the laser beams or whatever the hell they are?"

Holy fire of God . . . the sapphire staff I had almost forgotten. Joseph had it before I shot Delgado.

"The staff?" I questioned.

"In your bag upstairs, locked in the library," Joseph returned, an expression that held almost a sense of fear about whatever the staff was.

"Locked?"

"I used your keys. I couldn't think of any other place to put that thing," Joseph paused. "What is it anyway?" his frowning eyes stared at me.

"It's a long story," I whimpered.

Joseph gave me an exasperated questioning look.

"Maybe someday," I returned.

"Someday?" he scoffed. "Mel . . ." he started to protest.

"I'm too tired to deal with all the questions . . ." Which I was but I fained as much sympathy as I could. Explaining what the sapphire staff was meant explaining who I was and I wasn't nearly ready for that.

He snorted out softly. Looked at my bruised face and awkward leaning position and reasoned his questions could wait for a while. "You should be in bed," he said.

"I was hungry . . . I was going to get a piece of pie," I returned in the most pathetic tone I could muster.

"Fine," Joseph grumped and rolled his eyes. "I'll get you one."

"Bless you Joseph . . ."

He snorted with great distain and started into the kitchen.

Just then the office bell rang.

"I'll get it," I called out, wincing slightly at my raised voice.

"You can get the door but you can't get pie?" Joseph barked from the kitchen.

I ignored him and peered through the curtains. Miss Haptonstall stood at the front door. I timidly hobbled across the office in a slow shuffle.

"Miss Haptonstall, Emily," I said opening the door slowly to her in my robe.

I must have looked worse than I thought because her face turned slightly pale.

"Are you alright?" she asked with a pained sympathy that made me feel a little better. "That was kind of a dumb question . . . of course you're not . . . look at you . . ."

"I've been worse . . ." I said with a hunched and delayed wobble back into the living room, just as Joseph was returning with pie. Emily followed shutting and locking my office's front door behind her. "But I took care of Joseph . . ." I offered.

Joseph nearly jumped out of his skin as I startled him. I guess he was still a bit jumpy from the nerve trying evening.

"Miss Haptonstall," he recovered, sliding the pie back to the center of the plate. He had caught himself before dropping it on the floor.

I sat down gingerly on the sofa, taking one of the pieces of pie from Joseph.

"Pie?" Joseph offered, handing his piece to Emily and returned to the kitchen to retrieve another piece.

"Is this what you do?" she questioned staring at me, still with a note of deep sympathy in her steely blue eyes, her fingers gripping the small plate. "Fight Nazis then eat pie?"

I thought for a moment while I chewed then nodded. "Apple pie is very American." I could have made a connection to the town of Apple too but it lost something along the way, besides I was too worn out to be witty.

"Oh God that's a bad joke," she returned in a soft voice.

See. "No," I returned, as Joseph came in, ". . . me taking care of Joseph was a bad joke . . . Joseph took care of me . . ."

Joseph's face pinkened slightly as he sat down in the other chair, sticking a fork in his, I noticed, rather larger piece of pie.

"And Mr. Zalbowski?" Emily questioned turning from Joseph back to me.

"Here," Zalbowski said coming down the spiral staircase. His face was bruised and had some small nasty cuts on his jowls and forehead. His white shirt now tucked in still showed the signs of spattered dried spots of blood. His son, Jeffrey, followed holding his father's hand. The boy was small and thin with deep dark circles under his brown eyes, soft, warm brown puppy dog eyes, filled with a gentle sweetness like his father. His dark hair was straight but rumpled due no doubt to his curled sleeping position. The grip on his father's hand was tight, and tightened as he glanced fitfully around the unfamiliar room. I was able to see the little sinews and knuckles in his hand twist with tension. Mr. Zalbowski however was like a new man, even in his rumpled, stubbled appearance. For the past few days he had appeared lethargic, distraught, sad and angry. A man sullen in every demeanor except for his puppy dog eyes that pleaded for help and deliverance from his living hell. But now even with his battered features, now he was almost vibrant. Even his eyes were brighter. His step assured, his spine straight, his mind altered and if I said so myself he even looked a little thinner.

"I owe you all a huge debt. One I will not forget," he said shaking Joseph's hand as well as Emily's. I stood slowly to shake his.

Mr. Zalbowski however grabbed me in a great bear hug and with his short stance to me his arms wrapped right over my stitches.

I winced in pain but held my tongue from crying out.

"Thank you Mr. Taylor. If you need anything, anything ever please . . ."

Let me go I thought. "You're welcome Mr. Zalbowski . . ." I half sputtered as he finally released me.

"Isaac please," he said, his son once again grabbing his hand.

"Umm Isaac . . ." I paused half smiling at Jeffrey who buried his head in his father's side. "Can I . . . speak to you a minute . . ." I looked down at Jeffrey.

Zalbowski understood. The kid had been through enough. I didn't want to add to any future fears.

"Jeffrey sit right here . . ." his father smiled with a gentle embrace, having to softly pry his hand's release. "I'll be right there," he pointed to the open kitchen.

"Would you like a piece of pie," Emily offered up her uneaten one to the small boy as she sat down beside him with a kind smile.

"Mr. Zal . . . Isaac . . ." I started then hesitated. "About . . . Delgado and Cox . . ."

"Joseph told me some of it," he returned, his joy lessening.

"Isaac . . ." I started as he peered up at me. "Isaac . . . while I think those men were after me more than you . . . I can't guarantee there won't be things in the future . . . incidents, problems . . . it might be smart to move or . . . maybe even change your name . . . I might have stopped Delgado and Cox but . . ."

Zalbowski paused. "I won't run Mr. Taylor," his face serious as he looked at me. "I'm tired of being afraid . . . and more I will not let these men win. They wanted to make us anonymous, non-existent . . . simple numbers and statistics in their experiments. I won't do that. My father lived. I lived and now thanks to you my son lives . . ." It was obvious he had already thought of the future. His soft brown eyes glanced lovingly at Jeffrey on the sofa. "But now we know . . . we are no longer ignorant Mr. Taylor . . . and that is what they are afraid of the most, being known . . . if we know them their power diminishes, if we stand up to them their power diminishes . . . and someday when everyone knows . . . when everyone stands they will have no more power."

I smiled. He was right and for a moment he reminded me of an old friend. "If you have any problems . . ." I nodded. "If anyone or anything . . ."

He hugged me once more and I grimaced in pain.

"I'm sorry Mr. Taylor," he said pushing his spare retrieved pair of wire rimmed glasses up onto the bridge of his nose.

"Mel . . . call me Mel," I returned. "And if you ever need anything . . ."

"There is . . . . one small question . . ." Zalbowski began lowering his voice and turning away from the living room. "You . . . those men knew you . . . they called you Captain . . ." his brown eyes looked at me.

"We all have our pasts . . ." I said. ". . . some of them we'd like to forget . . ." I added, my voice expressing its request for tolerance at my desired omissions.

He nodded and didn't continue, perhaps too grateful to pursue it any further. "And that strange thing . . . the glowing blue stick . . . what is it?"

"That I'm afraid is also for another day . . ." I slowly returned.

"The man . . . Delgado . . . he called it the sapphire staff . . . is it? I mean could it be?" his eyes were wide with questioning as he peered up at me.

I raised an eyebrow. Surprised he had even made the connection. "You remembered that?"

"I thought I was about to be killed Mr. Taylor you tend to listen very closely to things around you . . . . is it . . . ? The rod of . . ."

"Perhaps someday I'll tell you the story," I stopped him.

"Then *it* is . . ." he said in an astounded lowered voice. "The actual one?" he questioned.

"As far as I know . . ." I replied.

"Amazing . . . unbelievable . . ." he gasped, his mind pondering the enormity of what I had just told him. "Yes someday you must tell me, and if I am so honored perhaps . . . let me see it when there are a few less . . . distractions."

"Check, no murderous gunmen around," I snarked.

Zalbowski chuckled.

I hadn't seen the man crack even the smallest smile now he was laughing and at my bad jokes. The guy was definitely in a better place now that his son was alive and safe. "My door is always open to you and your son . . . any problems . . . anything . . ."

"Thank you. It will take my son some time . . ." he looked at Jeffrey in my living room. The boy's eyes trained on his father as he sat contained and still on the sofa. ". . . but he is alive and that is what I prayed for . . ." Zalbowski returned. "My door is always open to you too . . . Mel."

"Your door . . ." Oh God his sliding glass door.

"Now . . ." Zalbowski smiled. "We are going to go home . . . my son and I together."

"Good . . ." I said patting him on the shoulder. "Oh, Mr. Zal . . . Zalbowski . . . I'm sorry about your sliding glass door," I returned with a feeble attempt to inform him of his house's property damage.

"My sliding glass door?" he questioned looking at me.

"Didn't I mention . . ." I gave him a goofy grin. I just hoped the bloody behemoth was gone and not a dead corpse on the patio. I'm sure he was . . . gone I mean . . . not still on the patio. The mess probably wasn't but . . .

Zalbowski shook his head. "Don't worry Mel . . . a door doesn't matter . . ." he smiled walking into the living room.

"There's a cab out front," Joseph offered as we entered.

"Yes, I called one earlier," Zalbowski returned. He took his son's hand. "This is all that matters to me . . ." he kissed his son on the crown of his head. "Thank you all . . ."

I nodded and watched as Zalbowski and his son left through my front office door to the waiting cab out front.

"It might matter . . ." I mumbled. ". . . that door's been broken for two days. He's probably got squirrels and cats and God knows what else in his house."

"I don't think he'll mind in the least," Emily said with a soft smile, watching the reunited father and son depart.

"And you Emily?" I questioned.

Joseph raised an eyebrow at my use of her first name as he munched on his dessert.

"I had to see if I was still employed," she smiled.

"Oh you're still employed," I answered, sitting gingerly back down on the sofa next to her.

"Good," she smiled again.

We stared at each other wordless for a moment then looked to Joseph. Who was finishing his piece of pie.

"What?" he questioned still chewing.

"I'll call you in a few days," I said turning to Emily. "With some work, when you finish you can bring it by the office . . . or I can pick it up."

"I can come to the office," she answered quickly as she rose from her seat next to me on the sofa. "Joseph," she said turning. ". . . and Mel . . . take care of yourselves."

"Yes ma'am," I smiled and pleasantly watched as she walked across my office to the front door and departed.

"Or I can pick it up . . ." Joseph chuckled with an implying tone.

"You'd pick up a piano if she asked," I returned with snark.

"Not necessarily," Joseph answered as I moved from the stiff sofa to softly collapse into the more comfortable leather chair. My concoctions were working. The pain was ebbing even Zalbowski's last hug hadn't been quite as exuberate as the first. "So are we going to talk about it?" Joseph questioned setting his empty plate on the coffee table.

"About what?"

"About what!" Joseph gawfed.

"About that thing in your library," Joseph pointed to the ceiling like it was an unseen presence in the house. "About your library, about exploding cars, Nazis, disappearing men and you getting thrown practically over a burning house . . ."

"Really I was thrown over the house?" I replied. I felt like it.

"Mel?"

"Look Joseph," I knew he hadn't heard Delgado and unless Zalbowski told him what he thought, which obviously he hadn't or Joseph would be asking, he didn't know all that much about what that *thing* in my library was. I didn't know how much I wanted to tell. How much I was comfortable to tell. I hadn't told anyone about who I was or where, rather, when I had come from . . . should I spill the whole thing and let Joseph in on my little secret . . . or keep him in the dark. By the look on his face he wasn't going to take no for an answer. I had to tell him something. He was a smart guy. He was going to eventually figure it out, at least some of it. "The thing upstairs well it's kind of hard to explain . . ." I started.

"Try," he insisted.

"Let's just say I got it from some bad people like Delgado and I don't intend to let them have it."

He glared at me. "And Delgado? How do you explain Delgado?

Is he the same Dr. Delgado Ernst that was at Auschwitz? Is that even possible? I saw him . . . he wasn't that old and Cox? He's supposedly the same doctor for Isaac and his kid. Are these guys living forever? Some sort of Nazi fountain of youth? And you . . . you seem to know them and they obviously know you . . ."

Should I tell him? I looked at Joseph. I trusted him. He had saved my life. I owed him. Yeah you do . . . so what are you going to do ruin the guy's life and tell him all the things you know. All the things that keep you awake at night. All the things you wish you could change but can't. And that was all before you knew Delgado was alive and maybe still kicking. The guy deserved some happiness . . . don't destroy that.

"Nah . . . Delgado and Cox were just playing. That wasn't really their names . . . just newbies playing at fascist neo-Nazi dreams of control and power . . . you know using old names to connect them to the glory of the past . . . as for . . . the thing upstairs . . . it's just a prototype some kind of ultra new weapon . . ." God I hope he bought this crap. Most people want a simple answer, but I'm really bad at lying.

"And what about the hospital and all the weird electronic stuff?" his frowning eyes were still staring at me.

"It's the staff when you use it . . . it messes up your whole body electricity . . . sorry about your car by the way."

"Cars," he clarified.

"Yeah cars."

"The SUV . . . I thought the bullet holes and the bent axial were enough but hey the electrical was screwed up too . . ." he breathed out a short breath. ". . . so a prototype weapon huh?" he sounded doubtful.

"Ah . . . yeah," I returned.

"How did I know how to work it?" he questioned looking at his hands as if he could still recall the presence of the staff on his skin.

"Ah . . . were you intending to blow up the cars?" I questioned.

"No but . . . the thing . . . I could feel it . . . it was weird . . ." he frowned. "You're sure it's a weapon?"

"I told you it messes up your body electricity." Which it did for me, but then I'd used it while blowing up a Nazi time device with a hand grenade.

"So am I a walking electrical box now too?"

"No . . ." because you didn't travel through time and try to kill yourself. ". . . you only used it a few seconds," I answered. "You'll be fine . . ."

"So how often do you use that thing?"

"Off and on." Not since 1948. "So . . . anything else?" I questioned hoping what I hadn't told him was enough.

"I don't know if I believe you . . ." Joseph returned.

That wouldn't surprise me.

"But I figure anybody who's stupid enough to risk their life for two friends and a bunch of kids can't be all that bad. Besides it will make one hell of an interesting investigation."

I frowned.

"I decided to start a new series of books. I've got several authors who have been following this proposed Nazi now scenario. So I'm throwing out a few leads to see who else is out there on the same subject . . . I do run an alternative science and history bookstore and publishing house. You wouldn't be interested in maybe expanding your resume and becoming an author?"

I was just relieved he was taking my bull so well. I shook my head. All the world needed was me trying to explain the things I'd seen in my longer than normal lifetime. "I've got enough excitement in my life."

"Yeah you do . . ." he said standing up.

"Hey Joseph," I said stopping him as he pushed the curtains, to my office, all the way back. "Thank you. You saved my life and those kids lives too."

"You want to thank me, pay my car bills, and come up with a better story than the one you just spun."

"Act of God, act of God . . ." I sputtered. ". . . besides technically you were driving both times."

"More like an act of Mel," he pointed to me.

I chuckled and Joseph pulled the curtains shut to the office obscuring my view.

"See yeah Mel," Joseph called passing the office desk. He paused. Miss Haptonstall's resume lay on top of the stack of papers. He took a quick glance before leaving out the front door. "What a load of crap," Joseph said stepping down the sidewalk. He knew there was a lot more to the story than what Mel had told him and he was going to find out what.

ොිඪ

I heard the front door shut. I knew Joseph didn't buy my explanation but I didn't care. He might want to know the truth but it didn't mean he was going to get it. He'd forget about it or find something else to occupy himself with after a while besides me and my insanity. I knew I should get up and lock the front door. But I figured the closed sign was out and after the past three days what else could possibly happen. I'd learned that even though I'd nearly killed myself and transported myself from 1948 to 1998 essentially skipping fifty years. My efforts hadn't been as successful as I thought. Dr. Eunholder had built two devices. The second I hoped I had destroyed last night. But the nagging feeling I was going to see Delgado and Cox again wasn't going away. I reassured myself with the consolation that I'd saved five people. Kept my friendships so far, only destroyed two cars and maybe, just maybe was settling down in this time after thirteen lost years of confusion and turmoil. Maybe I could finally have a life after all. I closed my eyes there was no place like home, regardless of the year.

EPILOGUE

"I'm so glad you could come, Mr. Taylor."

"Please Melburn, Mrs. Morgenstein," I replied greeting Joseph's mother for the first time. I had finally accepted her offer to dinner and had accompanied Joseph on his weekly Tuesday night dinner. Mrs. Morgenstein was still a quite pretty woman even for her weakened state. Her hair was fully white with a pronounced gentle curving curl that wrapped behind her ear. Joseph had told me some of her condition. She suffered from states of partial paralysis from which the doctors, all specialists, had not been able to diagnosis.

"Then you must call me Rebecca," she returned with a bright welcoming smile.

"Very well Rebecca, you have a very lovely home," I said, sitting down on a pale green love seat located in front of a large bay window that overlooked a terraced garden in the back yard. ". . . and an immaculate yard," I added feeling a tug on the still sensitive back wound. I had recuperated from my little adventure but I hadn't recovered completely.

"A benefit of having a son with a lawn maintenance business," she smiled. "He makes sure there's someone here everyday . . ." she lowered her voice. "I think it's more just so they can check up on me and make sure I don't need anything. It's Joseph's way of letting me be independent but taking care of me at the same time."

I smiled. It sounded like Joseph.

"Your son's a good man."

"He is. Like his father . . . it's a pity Jack never got to see Joseph's success," she replied with a tightened smile.

I looked at a picture on a small cherry side table, of a heavy set man with a shock of dark hair just like Joseph's.

"He died when Joseph was only twelve, a bad time for a young man to lose his father."

"But he turned out alright . . . thanks to you no doubt," I returned.

"Yes he did," she smiled. "And you Melburn . . . are your parents . . ." she started to inquire.

"I'm afraid they've both passed away." That tended to happen when you were technically just shy of one hundred.

"Both . . . oh I am sorry, and for someone so young . . . any siblings?"

"No," I answered feeling a bit uncomfortable for the first time.

"Joseph is an only child as well . . . I'm glad you two know each other . . . he's always working at his business. He seems to never have time for friends . . . or anything other than work . . ." there was a motherly note of future worry in her words.

Which business I thought, he owned three different ones. I heard a dish bang as it hit something in the kitchen.

"He insists on cooking every Tuesday and Friday," she said. "He always cooks more than I can eat so I have leftovers most of the week. Joseph tells me you're a genealogist," Rebecca turned back to me.

"Yes," I returned with a kind nod.

"It must be a fascinating profession."

"It can be."

"My husband did some family trees on the Morgenstein's. He had a large family, but I'm afraid my parents didn't talk much about the Lowen's"

"Lowen?" I questioned.

"Yes, Lowen was my maiden name."

"Dinner is served," Joseph announced entering the room with a flourish.

Lowen was an uncommon name and the fact that I had known someone with the name Lowen surprised me a bit. I wondered now what her father's name had been.

"Oh, Joseph you've out done yourself again," Rebecca said kissing her son on the cheek as he pulled out the chair for her to sit down. Joseph had prepared an entire salmon and large bowls of potatoes and peas with warm fresh rolls and butter. I had never realized Joseph had such culinary talents. I knew he could eat. In fact it was one of the main things he did when he was at my place. But as I watched Mrs. Morgenstein get to the table with a stuttered gait and obvious pain I understood why Joseph went to so much effort on the meal. He was a very good son.

Rebecca sat down accompanied by Joseph and myself a moment later. She lowered her head slowly as did Joseph and said a silent prayer. It was something I hadn't done over a meal in a very long time. I took a small silent moment myself. But it luckily didn't last long enough to allow my mind to wander.

Joseph began to serve taking his mother's plate first.

"I wanted to thank you Melburn, for the item you had my son purchase. It helped me a great deal," Rebecca began, as she made Joseph remove some of the mounding food from her plate until she approved of the correct amount.

I had told Joseph about a special ointment made by a gentleman of my acquaintance that helped to loose stiff muscles and joints with no adverse side effects like medications. I had discovered the guy when I'd been looking for seeds to start some of my . . . more special horticultural pursuits.

"I'm glad it helped," I returned, not at all offended by Joseph's generous heaping of my own plate.

The conversation remained light and humorous with Joseph telling us a recent publishing fiasco for the city. A sign they wanted printed that read dogs had to accompany all humans to the park and that humans must be leashed at all times. They had called the city to question the wording but they were assured it was as requested. Needless to say the city had reordered new signs that simply stated all dogs were to be leashed.

I noticed Rebecca staring at me quite intently at one moment through dinner but she said nothing. We continued on, adjourning finally to the living room while Joseph cleaned up. I offered to help but he insisted, so I returned to Rebecca and the pale green love seat.

"I'm sorry Melburn," she began after a long frowning stare once again. "But do you have relatives on the east coast?"

"No," I answered.

"It's strange you remind me of someone," she pondered my face a little longer shaking her head. "I'm sure it's just my old mind playing tricks with me . . . I was very young . . ."

"No my family was from here, this area," I returned then proceeded with my own curiosity. "Were the Lowen's from the east?"

"Oh yes, both my parents were born in New York State . . . so was I. We didn't move here until I was eight."

"Really . . ." I returned slightly intrigued.

"Oh yes, we lived in upper New York. It was a beautiful area with waterfalls and evergreens. I loved it as a child. The woods were so much different there than the Midwest. My father's work brought us here. He was an engineer and later an architect." She leaned forward slowly lifting a large photo album from the bottom of the coffee table. "I was the only one born in New York . . . my brothers were all born here." She rose and slowly came to sit down on the love seat next to me opening the photo album so I could see. There was a black and white photograph of a young girl with three much younger brothers. One of which was still a baby. "We were a very happy family," she said flipping through the album smiling at the different pictures. "There," she said stopping on a slightly larger photograph. "That's my mother and father."

My face betrayed my utter shock and I let out a puff of astonished air.

"Melburn?" Mrs. Morgenstein questioned noting my expression. "Are you alright?"

"Ester," I breathed out quietly.

"My mother . . . but how would you . . ." Rebecca half questioned looking at me closer. "Roy? . . . Roy!" she said with even more recognition.

I swallowed hard. I hadn't heard that name in years.

"Roy Taylor?" she couldn't look away from me now.

I looked back to the kitchen to make sure Joseph hadn't heard.

"It is you. I kept trying to think who you were . . . who you looked like . . . but . . . but," Rebecca stuttered. "How?"

I nodded my head. "You're Becca . . ." I held my hand up from the floor to show the height at which I last remembered her. "Ester's daughter . . . Joseph is Ester's grandson . . ." I couldn't believe it. "Is Ester?" I suddenly questioned a strange sense of hope in my words.

"My mother passed away five years ago," Rebecca replied, her eyes still staring at me with disbelief.

"Five . . . ah . . . Ester . . ." I had missed her.

"But how? How can you be the age you are . . . you're almost exactly as I remember," she shook her head, her features still in shock. "You were the one that told my parents to leave . . . it had something to do with my father's . . . his work . . . with Uncle Saul's work . . ."

Saul. I closed my eyes remembering my friend's last moments in pain.

"I remember my mother crying . . . that something had happened to Uncle Saul and we had to leave . . . that was when Daddy changed his name . . ."

I turned to look at Rebecca.

"My mother always called my father Jacob but when we came here she always called him James . . . she never called him Jacob again," she explained, looking back at the photograph before her.

"You had to go . . . I told Ester to leave . . . Ester . . ." I said emotions running hot under the surface of my skin. "I never thought she'd come here . . . I never thought . . . all those stories I told her . . . and Jacob . . ." I remembered Jacob.

"What happened to Uncle Saul . . . my mother never talked about him again. I think . . . I think it was just too painful for her," Rebecca questioned, her aged eyes looking at me. I could see the young child I'd known all those years ago, now imprisoned in the body of an elderly woman.

"It was too painful for all of us," I answered. I looked up to find Rebecca's eyes peering at me in question. "Saul . . ." I stopped, feeling my eyes start to well a bit and I fought them back. "Saul was my best friend . . . friend isn't a good enough description . . . he was like my brother . . . yes my brother," I paused. "We made it through the war together. But we were still with the government . . . Saul, Saul gave his life to protect me . . . to protect your mother and father . . . to protect you . . . to protect everyone . . ." And it hadn't been enough I thought. It hadn't been enough not when Delgado and Cox had been alive and might still be alive. An acid taste crested my throat. I swallowed it back down.

"But you?" she questioned. "How did you?"

"It was an accident. Something the government was working on, something that went . . . wrong. It needed to be stopped. Saul and I tried to stop it."

"I knew my father worked for the government and that some of it was top secret but . . ." Rebecca started.

"Does anybody want desert?" Joseph questioned, entering the living room again.

I couldn't look at him.

"Yes dear please," Rebecca returned not missing a beat, allowing Joseph to return to the kitchen.

"Don't tell Joseph please . . ." I said under my breath, looking back at her.

Rebecca slowly nodded a sad expression on her face. I looked back toward the kitchen waiting for Joseph. He was Ester's grandson.

"Roy . . . Melburn . . ." Rebecca corrected herself. "Here," she said offering me a small black and white photograph. I could see the page in the album where she had just removed it.

I looked down at it. It was Ester, Saul and myself. The year before he'd died. The year before, I was thrown into the future. The year before Dr. Eunholder's device, the year our lives had still held some semblance of meaning.

Joseph returned and I quickly slipped the photograph into my pocket. That was why . . . why I thought, taking the piece of cake and handing it to Rebecca . . . that was why when Joseph picked up the sapphire staff it functioned. Why he was able to wield it. Joseph handed me a piece of cake. Joseph was Ester's grandson, but more importantly he was Saul's direct relative.

The Sapphire Staff Series
will continue with

Book Two

DR. EUNHOLDER'S DEVICE